E

SILVER FRUIT UPON SILVER TREES

It would be easy, Eve told Sophie. All she had to do was to go to Trinidad and pretend to be the granddaughter of the wealthy Brandt St. Vincente for four weeks and the money she needed would be hers. But when Sophie met the disturbing Edge St. Vincente, who thought she was his niece, and fell in love with him, she realised that perhaps it wasn't going to be that simple after all . . .

SILVER FRUIT
UPON SILVER TREES

BY

ANNE MATHER

MILLS & BOON LIMITED
17-19 FOLEY STREET
LONDON W1A 1DR

First published 1974
This edition 1974

© Anne Mather 1974

ISBN 0 263 716058

Made and Printed in Great Britain by
C. Nicholls & Company Ltd.
The Philips Park Press, Manchester

The publishers wish to thank The Literary [...] of Walter de la Mare, and the Society of A[...] their representative, for permission to qu[...] poem 'Silver'.

CHAPTER ONE

SOPHIE thought she must have been mad to agree to come. What was she doing here in Port of Spain, waiting with palpitating heart for Eve's grandfather to come and fetch her? How could she hope to play this role so well that no one would suspect she was not Eve Hollister? Wasn't it a criminal offence to impersonate someone else? Or did that apply when the person involved had given her permission, indeed had begged her to do it? Sophie gave a helpless little shrug. Her palms were moist, a rivulet of pure sweat was running into the small of her back, a damp trembling unsteadiness seemed to have invaded her legs. She paced restlessly about the hotel room trying to calm her nerves, going over and over in her mind the things Eve had impressed upon her.

She had nothing to worry about, she told herself, but without much conviction. The St. Vincentes had never seen Eve, so how could they possibly know what she looked like, know anything about her other than what she had chosen to tell them in her letters? And after all, she and Eve did have similar characteristics. They were both blonde to begin with, but whereas Eve's hair had a silvery lightness, Sophie's was corn-gold with streaks of a darker shade. They were both slightly above average height, slim, and if Sophie's slimness was slightly more pronounced, that was because she hadn't always paid enough attention to food. But there had been so many more important things on which to spend the small salary she earned as stage manager and general dogsbody of the Pier Playhouse in Sandchurch that looking after herself had not figured highly amongst them. Eve had thought she was crazy slaving away for such a pittance, but then Eve had never known what it was to have financial problems.

Sophie had first met Eve four years ago when she was eighteen and in her first job in London. Although becoming an actress had always been her first choice for a career she had been sensible enough to realize that she would need some other means to support herself. Consequently, she had taken a course in shorthand and typewriting and had been at that time working in the typing pool of one of the independent television companies.

Eve was a journalist, a young and successful journalist, who had already made quite a name for herself in Fleet Street. Sophie had been seconded to her when she came to do an article about the television company, and the two girls had become friends right away. Whether it was that they were so similar in age – Eve was only three years older than Sophie – or whether Sophie's extreme unsophistication in the face of Eve's worldliness attracted them to one another neither could say, but from the beginning they had enjoyed each other's company. Thus it was that when Sophie confided her desire to become an actress to Eve, she had used her influence to get Sophie the chance of stage manager at the Sandchurch Playhouse. Of course, Sophie had realized that Eve did not really expect her to stick at it, but she had, and for the past three and a half years she had been happy in her own way. She hadn't had a lot of money, but she had made some good friends, and from time to time there had been a weekend in London with Eve to look forward to.

Eve seemed to lead a much more exciting life than Sophie, despite the younger girl's association with the theatre. Eve was always being invited to parties or having all-expenses-paid holidays covering some feature or other. She had lots of boy-friends and never seemed to spend much time with her father, who Sophie knew was retired and lived alone in Kensington. She had casually mentioned that her mother had died when she was born, and she felt her father had never really forgiven her for being the cause of her mother's death.

To Sophie, brought up by an elderly aunt, this was a tragic situation. She had never known what it was to have parents, and she felt sure that in the same circumstances she would have had to have tried to show her father that because there were just the two of them they should mean more to one another. But it was not her affair and aside from mentioning occasionally that she thought that Eve ought to visit with her father more often, there was nothing she could do.

Then about six months ago Eve's father had died. She had attended the funeral accompanied by Sophie, and afterwards had confided that she supposed she would have to let her mother's family know. This was the first Sophie had heard of Eve's mother's family, and she had been fascinated when she had learned that they were wealthy plantation owners in Trinidad. The further information that Eve's mother had run away to marry James Hollister when she was only eighteen years old had explained why, until then, Sophie had never heard Eve mention them. But now the whole story came out. Eve's father had been an engineer, working on a constructional job in Trinidad,

9

when he and her mother met. Compared to the wealthy St. Vincente family, James Hollister had been considered a very poor match, and besides, Eve's mother was already engaged to the son of another of the wealthy families on the island.

But, rather cynically, Eve had gone on to explain that it was love at first sight, and the young couple had run away to England and never returned to Trinidad. Of course, her grandfather had cut off his daughter completely, and not even the knowledge that she had died in childbirth had softened the hardness of his heart. Eve's father was heartbroken at the death of his wife, and apart from ensuring that Eve was well cared for, he had paid little attention to her. She had grown up with a series of nannies, progressed through boarding school, and had finally displayed the fine talent for writing which had enabled her to obtain one of the highest paid posts in British journalism.

Sophie had heard nothing more about the St. Vincentes until a few weeks ago when Eve invited her to spend a weekend at her flat. Then she had confessed that she had been corresponding with her grandfather for the past few months. He must have softened with the years, because he had replied almost by return to her brief missive concerning her father's death, and since then he had written several times.

Sophie had been delighted at this news. She had thought that at last Eve was to know the pleasure of belonging to a real family. But, as usual, Eve was unpredictable.

She admitted that in the beginning the idea of effecting a reconciliation with her mother's family had amused her, but now her grandfather had suggested that she should go to Trinidad, to their house at Pointe St. Vincente, and spend several weeks getting to know her relatives.

"Can you imagine it, darling?" she had asked Sophie, with that wide-eyed stare which men seemed to find so appealing. "Me, cutting myself off from civilization for several weeks! Heavens, I'd go mad! I really would."

Sophie had not known what to say. She had been able to understand Eve's consternation in one way. She was simply not the type to exist without the hectic whirl of her present life, but on the other hand she had written to her grandfather and virtually invited just this situation.

"So what do you intend to do?" she had asked at last, and that was when Eve had exploded her bombshell.

"I thought you might like to go instead of me, Sophie," she said, and before giving Sophie a chance to utter any protest, she went on: "Don't say no straight away. Give it some thought."

Sophie drew a deep breath. "You can't be serious!"

"Why not?"

"Well, because – because it's impossible!"

"Why is it impossible?"

Sophie's eyes searched Eve's face for some sign of amusement, some indication that this was all just a joke and not to be taken seriously. "Eve –"

"Listen to me, Sophie. Didn't you tell me a few weeks ago that Roderick Harvey was holding an actors' summer school in Rome later this year?"

"*Sir* Roderick Harvey," corrected Sophie automatically.

"All right then, Sir Roderick Harvey. Well? Isn't he?"

"Y–es, yes, of course."

"Well, how would you like to attend?"

"Me?" Sophie stared at her friend in amazement. "Attend the summer school?"

"Yes. I – er – I could arrange it."

"I couldn't afford it," stated Sophie flatly.

"I could."

"Oh, Eve, for heaven's sake, what are you trying to say? That if I go out to Trinidad in your place you'll arrange for me to go to Roderick Harvey's summer school?"

"That's right."

Sophie was flabbergasted. "But why? Why should you do that?"

Eve had risen to her feet then and paced barefooted about the soft carpet of her lounge. "Does there have to be a reason? We're friends, aren't we? I thought we could help one another without there having to be too many reasons why."

Sophie stretched her legs out in front of her. "You know I'd do anything to help you, Eve, but this – well, this is something different."

"How is it different?"

"You know how." Sophie examined a tiny hole in her tights, trying not to think about what she was turning down.

"I don't." Eve leant negligently against the mantel. "Here I am, offering you not only the chance to attend this summer school you've been enthusing about but also several weeks' holiday on one of the most exciting islands in the world. I'd have thought you'd jump at the chance! "

"Would you?" Sophie's tone was dry.

"Yes, I would. Honestly, Sophie, where's your spirit of adventure? Don't you want to see something of the world before you're too old to appreciate it? You're not going to get anywhere at that third-rate playhouse in Sandchurch!"

Sophie flushed. "The Playhouse is not third-rate. And I'm glad you reminded me that I'm employed there!"

"You could get leave of absence." Eve was impatient. "You're not indispensable, you know."

She could be cruel when opposed, Sophie had learned that earlier in their relationship, and she tried not to be hurt by the things Eve was saying. She realized it was just her way of trying to make Sophie change her mind, and she returned her attention to her legs, curving one foot to rest against the ankle bone of the other.

Eve seemed to realize that her present tactics were getting her nowhere, for she sighed and then said apologetically: "I'm sorry, Sophie. I'm a bitch. But I was really depending on you to get me out of this."

Sophie looked up. "Out of what?"

Eve shrugged, reaching for a pack of cigarettes. She offered them to Sophie, but she refused. She smoked only very occasionally, and usually when she was suffering from nervous tension on the first night of a play.

"I've virtually agreed to go to Pointe St. Vincente," confessed Eve, lighting her cigarette with a monogrammed gold lighter.

"But why?" Sophie was astounded.

Eve shrugged. "Oh, you know how it is. One starts something like this and pretty soon it gets out of hand."

"But you must have known whether or not you intended going to Trinidad!" declared Sophie.

"You don't understand. The letters my grandfather has written to me have sort of – assumed that I would

13

want to go there. It's obvious he regrets very much what happened twenty-five years ago and he'd like the chance to make amends. I suppose he sees me orphaned and alone, without any family of my own now that my father is dead."

"Well, that's true."

"Yes, but not in the way he believes. I mean – the very last thing I need is some doting parent checking on my movements!"

Sophie sighed. Obviously the image Eve's grandfather had of her was vastly different from the original.

"You'll just have to write and tell him that your work won't permit you to have leave at this time," she suggested practically.

"No, I don't want to do that." Eve was resolute.

"Why?"

"Well – don't be cross if I tell you."

"If you tell me what?" Sophie cupped her chin in her hands.

Eve considered the glowing tip of her cigarette. "Well, they don't know I'm a journalist –"

"What?"

Eve made a dismissive gesture. "It's true. It was a sort of game I played."

"A game?"

"Yes." Eve hesitated. "When I first wrote to tell Grandfather about my father's death, I didn't mention my career, and when he wrote back to me it was obvious that he thought I was – well, you know – some sort of clerk. So I let him go on thinking it."

"But why?" Sophie was astounded.

"Oh, if I'd told him I was a journalist, I guess I'd have ruined the image."

"In what way?"

"Well, journalists – women journalists particularly – are usually very competent, self-confident types. Hard, if you like. I just knew that my grandfather wouldn't respond to anyone like that, so I pretended to be a secretary."

"Oh, Eve!"

Eve shrugged. "So what? I might well have been."

"But what has that got to do with you going out there?"

"My grandfather is an old man. My letters have made him happy. They've reassured him, if you like. If I refuse to go out there now, can't you see what it would do to him?"

Sophie hunched her shoulders. Of course. She could see quite well. This old man had clung to the small comfort of Eve's letters. He had built his hopes up of seeing her, of possibly spending some of his last days with her. How could she disappoint him now?

Sophie was aware of Eve's eyes upon her and with a helpless shrug she said: "You'll have to go."

"But I can't."

"You mean you won't."

"No, I mean I can't. Apart from anything else, I have this assignment coming up. John Fellowes; you know John Fellowes, don't you?" Sophie had heard of him and she nodded, and Eve went on: "Well, John and I have been offered the chance to go to the Middle East. The paper wants to do a series of articles about Middle-Eastern statesmen, and if it's successful who knows where it will lead? There's been talk of a television series –"

"Wait a minute, wait a minute!" Sophie held up a protesting hand. "This has nothing to do with me. The trip sounds great – the Middle Eastern trip, I mean, but so far as your grandfather is concerned –"

"Darling, would you deny me the chance to work with John? It's what I've been angling for for years –"

"Eve, It's nothing to do with me! You simply can't have your cake and eat it. You'll have to choose."

There was silence for a long time and then Eve said slowly: "And I thought you were my friend."

"I am your friend." Sophie sounded exasperated.

"Friends help one another. Like I helped you when you wanted to leave the typing pool and join a repertory company."

Sophie stared at her in disbelief. "But that was altogether different."

"How was it? Without my help you'd probably still be pounding the typewriter. Making your own way in the theatre world is no sinecure."

"I know that, but – but –"

"But what? But you'd have made it anyway?"

"I didn't say that." Sophie felt shocked. "Eve, do you realize what you're asking me to do?"

"Yes, I realize. I'm asking you to spend a few weeks on a plantation in the West Indies pretending to be me, and in so doing helping an old man to die happy."

"You make it sound so easy!"

"It is easy. Where's the problem? They've never met me. They know nothing about me except what I've chosen to write in my letters. You say you want to be an actress. Well, here's a chance to prove you can do it. And

16

there's still the summer school in Rome to look forward to later."

Sophie pressed her fingers through the long thick hair which fell about her slim shoulders. "You're making things terribly difficult for me, Eve," she admitted.

Eve pressed home her advantage. She came to kneel before Sophie, taking her hands in both of hers and saying: "Darling, I don't want to blackmail you into doing this, but can't you see — you can do it! Don't you want to be responsible for bringing a little happiness into Brandt St. Vincente's life?"

Sophie blinked. "Brandt St. Vincente? Is that your grandfather's name?"

Eve nodded.

"Do you have a — a grandmother?"

Eve shook her head. "No, she died about ten years ago."

"And this old man — does he live alone?"

"No. There's his son, my mother's brother, Edge."

"Edge?" Sophie tried not to become interested. "He lives with your grandfather?"

"Yes."

"He's not married?"

"He's a widower. I imagine he's my grandfather's manager. He must be middle-aged now."

"Is — is that the whole ménage?"

"No. There's my great-aunt Rosalind, generally known as Rosa, I believe. That's how my grandfather used her name in the letters."

"I see." Sophie released one hand and pushed back her hair from her face. "And that's all?"

"As far as I know. And after all, you'll be expected to

know no more than what was written in the letters. You can read them if you like. Then you'll see it all first-hand."

"No, thanks." Sophie felt a sense of distaste. Eve's grandfather had written those letters in good faith. He had not expected them to be shown around to her friends.

Eve looked impatiently at her. "Well?" she urged. "Will you do it?"

Sophie shook her head. "I don't know, I honestly don't know. Give me time to think about it."

But of course she had eventually given in, as Eve had known she would. Sophie tried to tell herself that her motives were mainly concerned with saving Brandt St. Vincente from disappointment, but deep down she despised the knowledge that the proposed visit to the Actors' Summer School had helped to persuade her.

And now here she was in the hotel room in Port of Spain, waiting with impatience for Eve's grandfather to come and greet his long-lost granddaughter. It had been Eve's idea to wait until she was actually in Port of Spain before contacting the St. Vincentes. That way it avoided the awkwardness of passports and so on at the airport. Sophie had been amazed at the deviousness Eve could display when called upon to do so, and she was beginning to wonder how well she had known the other girl all these years.

She went to the window now and looked out on the busy street below her. Eve had insisted that she book into one of the better known hotels, and this one was in the very heart of the city. It was also alarmingly expensive and Sophie wondered how long her money would last out if she had to stay here longer than expected. From the window, the bustling throng of humanity outside frightened her a little. She was not a seasoned traveller and nor was she an extrovert, and the knowledge that she knew no one amongst all these people of so many different colours and nationalities was rather terrifying.

There were Indian women in saris, American men in Hawaiian shirts and straw hats; dhotis and turbans, lace mantillas and fezes. She saw beautiful olive-skinned Chinese girls in gorgeously patterned cheongsams slit daringly to thigh level, and black African women carrying enormous bundles on their heads with casual elegance. Car horns blared impatiently, bicycle bells jangled, and those who were brave enough to board the gaily painted buses clung carelessly to the rails and seemed to jump on and off wherever they liked. To Sophie the whole scene breathed an excitement and exuberance from which she felt totally alienated.

Suddenly the telephone beside the bed shrilled loudly. Sophie almost jumped out of her skin. She turned back to look at it, both hands pressed to her mouth, and felt a genuine sense of panic assail her. The only people who knew she was here in Port of Spain were the St. Vincentes, so this call had to be something to do with them. All of a sudden she was sure she couldn't go through with it and she heard the phone ringing and ringing through the waves of unreasoning fear that swept over her.

The phone eventually stopped ringing and the silence which followed brought her inevitably to her senses. Her hands fell loosely to her sides and she drew long trembling breaths, trying to calm her shaken nerves. She should have answered it, she told herself fiercely. What if the telephonist chose to check up on who was in room

75? What if she discovered that it was not Miss Hollister after all, but Miss Slater? Sophie's heart thumped violently, and she quickly crossed the room to seat herself on the side of the bed and lift the telephone receiver. This had been another of Eve's devious ideas: to book into a hotel large enough not to remember the names of all their guests, and then to give a room number in her communication with the St. Vincentes. Naturally, she had had to take a room in her own name. They had wanted to see her passport. But what if right now they were flicking through their records, telling whoever it was who was trying to contact her that there was no one called Hollister registered in the hotel?

When the telephonist answered, Sophie said: "Were you ringing me? I'm afraid I was – in the bathroom."

"Miss Hollister?" asked the telephonist politely.

Sophie crossed her fingers. "Yes."

"There is an extension in the bathroom, Miss Hollister," the telephonist advised her smoothly. Then: "We have been trying to locate you. There's a gentleman in the foyer waiting to see you. A Mr. St. Vincente."

St. Vincente! The name threatened to destroy all her new-found confidence. And he was here, in the foyer! She had not expected him to come without calling first.

Managing to keep her voice calm, she said: "I – I see. Er – I'll come down. Gi – give me five minutes."

"Very well, Miss Hollister. I'll tell Mr. St. Vincente you'll be down directly."

"Thank you."

Sophie replaced the receiver and looked down at the simple cotton dress she was wearing. Was this the sort of garment Eve might have worn to meet her grandfather for the first time? Or ought she to change into something a little more formal? She shrugged. Eve would not want her to behave any differently from usual, and the pale blue dress looked cool and attractive against her pale skin.

With a sigh she rose to her feet and walked to the dressing table, examining her face in the mirror there. Her cheeks did look very pale, and her grey eyes seemed to be reproaching her for what she was about to do. But it was too late now. She was here. She was committed.

At the end of the rubber-tiled corridor outside her room, a row of lifts gave access to the ground floor. A dark-skinned West Indian boy smiled at her when she chose to enter his small cage and commented cheerfully upon the weather as they descended the six floors between them and the foyer.

When she walked into the foyer she was trembling, but she had to go on. She crossed to the reception desk covertly examining the men she could see standing about in groups or singly, but none of them seemed old enough to be Eve's grandfather.

The receptionist of the moment was a slim young Indian who smiled encouragingly at Sophie when she approached him.

"I'm – I'm Miss Hollister," she said in a low voice. "I understand there's someone waiting to see me."

"Oh, yes, Miss Hollister." The young man nodded. "Mr. St. Vincente is waiting for you in the Kingston Bar."

"The Kingston Bar," echoed Sophie faintly. "Where – where's that?"

"Through the archway, miss. You'll see the sign on your right."

"Oh! Oh, thank you."

Sophie nodded her thanks and turned away from the desk. The Kingston Bar! Hardly the place she would have expected an old man to wait for his long-lost grand-daughter, but that was hardly her affair. And how on earth was she to recognize him?

She walked to the archway the young Indian had indicated and looked about her. There were several illuminated signs directing guests to the various different facilities of the hotel and the one indicating the Kingston Bar was easy to find. Everything about the hotel breathed the kind of luxury she had never until now experienced, and the Kingston Bar was no exception. Even at this early hour of the evening there were a number of guests partaking of pre-dinner drinks in the secluded booths set between trellises of climbing plants, vivid with flamboyant blossom. The bar was artificially lit by old ships' lanterns which cast a shadowy gloom into certain corners inducing an intimate atmosphere, while the bar itself was strung with coloured lights which glinted in the shiny black face of its Trinidadian tender.

Sophie looked down again at her unsophisticated cotton dress. She should have changed, she thought unhappily. After all, it was almost dinner time and the women she could see were all dressed with the ultimate amount of care.

She looked about her helplessly. Where was Eve's grandfather? Surely he ought to have been waiting near the entrance to the bar, watching for her. But there was no one near the entrance, no one who appeared to be alone at all except a dark man seated on a tall stool at the bar with a tall glass of some amber-looking liquid before him.

Even as her eyes lingered on him the man turned his head and looked her way and a shiver of pure apprehension ran through her. He was easily the most devastatingly attractive male she had ever seen in her life, although she realized there was something cruel in the thin line of his mouth and a sardonic appreciation of the effect he had upon women in the cynical depths of his eyes. They were strange amber-coloured eyes, reflecting the colour of the liquid in the glass he raised to his lips, and they moved over Sophie with insolent consideration.

She looked away from him quickly. She was not used to being assessed in that manner and she didn't like it. Where on earth was Brandt St. Vincente? Why didn't he come forward and introduce himself? Surely if he was here, he could see her standing there obviously waiting for someone?

The man at the bar slid off his stool, swallowed a mouthful of his drink, made a casual comment to the bartender and then walked toward her. Sophie's pulses raced alarmingly, and she half turned away. Heavens, she thought in dismay. He thinks I'm on the lookout for a man!

"Eve?" The attractive male voice spoke somewhere near her temple.

She gasped and spun round again. The man from the bar was standing negligently before her, one hand brushing the jacket of his immaculate dark brown silk suit aside to rest on his hip just above the low waistband of his trousers, his other arm hanging casually at his side. Close to he was even more disturbing than before, and Sophie could hardly formulate the words she wanted to say. His hard body, lean and muscled, was only inches away from

23

hers, his lazy intelligent eyes were regarding her with vague mockery, and he emanated an aura of latent strength and virility.

"I – I think you've made a mistake –" she was beginning, when he interrupted her.

"You are – Eve Hollister, are you not?" he queried, dark eyebrows lifting sardonically.

Sophie stared at him. "Well – yes, I'm Eve Hollister. But – but who are you?"

He straightened. "My name is Edge St. Vincente. Surely my father mentioned me."

"*Edge* –" Sophie brought herself up short. "You were – I mean – you're my mother's brother?"

"I believe I have that privilege." She had the feeling he was enjoying her consternation.

"Then – then are you the – the Mr. St. Vincente who – who is waiting for me?" Eve could scarcely take it in. This man was Edge St. Vincente, the brother of Eve's dead mother, the man Eve had described to Sophie as being a widower of middle age!

She shook her head. Edge St. Vincente wasn't middle-aged. She doubted he was much over thirty-five, and she had the feeling that the experience in those strange amber eyes of his had not been put there by his wife.

CHAPTER TWO

"THAT is correct," Edge St. Vincente was saying now. "Who were you expecting?"

Sophie gathered her scattered wits. "I – I thought – my grandfather –"

"Oh, I see." Edge inclined his head. "Well, no. I'm sorry to disappoint you, but my father seldom visits Port of Spain. He doesn't care for the – er –" he glanced round expressively, shrugging, "– the atmosphere of the place."

"I see." Sophie pressed her hands together.

Edge returned his attention to her, studying her intently, bringing the hot colour to her pale cheeks. "So you're Eve. You don't look much like your mother."

Sophie tried to return his gaze. "I suppose I must take after my father."

"I suppose." His expression had become brooding. "Well –" He looked towards the bar. "Shall we have a drink?"

Sophie hesitated. "I don't – drink much."

"Don't you?" Again the dark brows were lifted. "I thought all newspaper women enjoyed the social side of their work."

"Newspaper women?" Sophie was really shocked now and she couldn't hide it.

"Yes." Edge turned back towards the bar and she had perforce to fall into step beside him. "You are a reporter, aren't you? Or is that some other Eve Hollister?"

Sophie felt shattered. In one sentence Edge St. Vincente had destroyed the whole image Eve had so painstakingly built around her. They ought to have realized that a family like the St. Vincentes would not accept a stranger into their midst without first checking up on her. But how much checking up had been done? And by whom?

She chanced a swift sideways glance at her companion. He seemed relaxed enough. There had been no censure in his remark. But how could she tell? All her old fears came to haunt her. She should not have given in to Eve; she should not have agreed to come. She ought to have known that she could never get away with it.

They had reached the bar and Edge indicated that she should take one of the tall stools while he attracted the attention of the barman. Sophie climbed on to the stool with some misgivings, trying desperately to think of some reply to make.

Edge sat easily on the stool beside her, his arms resting on the bar. He was much taller than she was and had not had the difficulty getting on to his seat that she had had. He summoned the bartender and when he came he ordered himself another Bacardi and Coke and then looked quizzically at Sophie.

"Well?" he urged her. "What's it to be?"

Sophie ran her tongue over dry lips. "Perhaps — a sherry?" she suggested.

"Sherry?" He sounded amused. "All right. And a sherry, too, Gene."

"Yes, sir, Mr. St. Vincente."

The bartender grinned and moved away to get their drinks. Sophie rested her hands on the bar to stop them from fidgeting. She glanced nervously round the dimly lit area, and shifted rather awkwardly on her stool. She

26

wondered whether he was aware of her extreme state of tension. She thought it was likely.

He drew out a long case of cigars and regarded them thoughtfully. "I'm afraid I can't offer you a cigarette, but Gene can give you some if you need them."

"I – I don't smoke."

"Don't you now?" His eyes narrowed as he placed a thick cigar between his teeth. "Curiouser and curiouser."

Sophie was convinced he was playing some sort of cat and mouse game with her. She opened her mouth to say that he had no need to say anything else. She admitted the truth; she was not Eve Hollister and she intended leaving Trinidad as soon as she could possibly get a flight.

But the words were never uttered, because he said: "I suppose you should call me Uncle, shouldn't you?"

Sophie's fingers curled into her palms. "I – I – if you like."

Edge St. Vincente was serious now, the mockery gone from his eyes. "It's what my father will expect," he stated quietly, lighting his cigar with a gold lighter. "But whether or not you choose to use the definition is, I suppose, up to you."

The bartender, Gene, returned with their drinks. He put them down and then rubbed the bar nearby with a damp cloth as though waiting for something more. Edge nodded his thanks, and then said: "You tell your brother-in-law to give me a call. I'll see what I can do."

"Yes, sir." Gene's face broke into a wide grin. "I'd sure be grateful, Mr. St. Vincente."

"That's okay." Edge gave a gesture of dismissal and the bartender moved away to attend to another customer. Then Edge turned his attention back to Sophie. "Now:

27

tell me. Did you have a good flight?"

Sophie's fingers curved round the stem of her glass as though it was a lifeline. "Yes, thank you," she replied quickly. She was about to go on and say that she had not done enough flying to know what was good and what was not, but she was wary now of what he might know and Eve was used to taking trips to the continent. "I – the flight landed late last night."

"Yes." Edge swallowed a mouthful of the Barcardi and Coke. There was a slice of lemon cut and draped to the side of his glass and he took it off and squeezed its juice into the spirit. The action drew attention to his hands, long-fingered brown hands, totally unlike the hands of any farmer Sophie had ever seen. But then the St. Vincentes were not ordinary farmers, were they? "My father was delighted to receive your telegram. You should have let us know the time of your flight and someone could have met you at the airport."

"I – I knew it would be so late in arriving. I thought it would be easier . . ." Sophie's voice trailed away. She sipped her sherry. This was only the beginning, she told herself severely. It was going to get much harder than this.

"Never mind." Edge let her off the hook. He drew on his cigar, exhaling a delicious aroma of Havana tobacco around them. "You're here now, and that's what matters, isn't it?"

"Yes." Sophie wished she felt as confident. "I – er – how far is it to – to your home?"

"Pointe St. Vincente?" He shrugged. "About thirty miles; north of here and along the coast."

"Oh, yes." Sophie looked into her drink. "I – I'm looking forward to meeting my – my grandfather."

28

"I expect you are." Edge's eyes were unnervingly penetrating. "Are you ready to leave?"

"Now?"

"In a few minutes."

Sophie thought of the hotel bill, made out in Sophie Slater's name. Her heart thumped uncomfortably loudly. Couldn't he hear it too?

"If – if you'll wait here, I'll go and collect my things," she said.

"All right." Edge finished the Bacardi and Coke, and summoned Gene again. "I'll have another."

Sophie slid off the stool. "I shan't be long."

"You haven't finished your sherry."

"Oh! Well, I'm not very thirsty."

His eyes narrowed. "Very well. I'll wait here."

Sophie nodded and hurried out of the Kingston Bar. In the hotel foyer she looked hopefully towards the reception desk and her silent prayers were answered. The Indian receptionist had gone and in his place was a dark-skinned West Indian girl she had not seen before. Sophie went up to her and explained who she was and that she would be leaving in a few minutes. The girl was polite and understanding. She agreed to have the bill ready and waiting when she came downstairs again after collecting her belongings.

The lift seemed to take aeons to reach the seventh floor and her key stuck in the lock and wouldn't immediately turn. It seemed to take her ages to gather her things together and reach the foyer again, and she was amazed to discover she had only taken fifteen minutes.

Leaving her suitcase in the charge of a bellhop, she quickly crossed the foyer to the reception desk.

A swift glance around had assured her that Edge St. Vincente was nowhere to be seen, and when the girl presented her bill Sophie paid it without even bothering to check it. Then she turned back towards the bar.

Edge St. Vincente was still seated at the long bar, but now he was not alone. A woman was draped on the stool which Sophie had previously occupied, a slim red-haired woman dressed in a long chiffon gown in shades of yellow. Sophie approached them nervously. Neither of them appeared to have noticed her presence and she didn't quite know whether she ought to interrupt. The woman had her back to the entrance, but Edge had not, and just when Sophie was considering turning away he caught sight of her and slid abruptly off his stool. Casting a wry glance at his companion, he said: "Here is my niece now, Sandra. Eve Hollister. Eve, come and be introduced to an old friend of mine."

As Sophie approached the woman turned rather languidly in her seat, resting an elbow in the bar to support herself. She was older than Sophie had at first imagined, about thirty, she thought, but maturity had added to rather than detracted from her beauty. There was something vaguely oriental about her classically moulded features, and she gave Edge a slanted glance from between slightly almond-shaped lids that belied a wholly European ancestry.

"I didn't know you were an uncle, darling," she murmured.

"Didn't you?" Edge half smiled. "Well, one learns a little something every day."

"Does Piers know he has a cousin?"

"I imagine he's as aware of that fact as anyone," returned Edge smoothly. Then, as though realizing that Sophie was standing listening to this with a certain amount of perplexity, he said: "Eve, allow me to present Mrs. March. Her husband and I share an interest in a small company on the southern coast of the island."

"How do you do?"

Sophie shook hands with Sandra March rather reluctantly. There was something about the older woman which repulsed her a little, although she wasn't quite sure what. It couldn't have anything to do with the rather proprietorial looks she was bestowing on Edge St. Vincente. His private affairs were nothing to do with Sophie. All the same, she didn't think it was right that a married woman should treat any man but her husband with such provocative intimacy.

"So you're Jennifer's daughter." Sandra March spoke consideringly. "And is Brandt killing the proverbial fatted calf in your honour?"

"Brandt?" For a moment Sophie felt blank. "Oh, you mean – my grandfather."

"That's right. He must be softening in his old age. He always swore he'd never forgive your mother for what she did."

"That's enough, Sandra." Edge's tone was incisive, and Sophie was amazed at the way his words could explode Sandra's bubble of confidence. "Now, you must excuse us. We have to be going."

Sandra put long fingers with purple lacquered nails on the fine material of his sleeve. "Oh, Edge darling, surely you can stay in town for dinner," she appealed.

"I'm afraid not." Edge moved so that her hand fell to her side.

31

"But it's ages since I've seen you —"

"I'm sorry, Sandra."

Sandra compressed her lips and looked coldly in Sophie's direction. "Aren't you lucky you're only his niece," she asked, with scarcely veiled sarcasm. "He's such a pig where women are concerned, aren't you, darling?"

Edge ignored her and looked compellingly at Sophie. "Are you ready?"

Sophie nodded. "Yes. One of the bellboys is looking after my suitcase in the foyer." She spoke quickly, wanting to get away, conscious of the other woman's humiliation, almost pitying her for it.

"Good. You go ahead. I'll be with you in a moment."

As she walked towards the doorway, Sophie heard the brief interchange between them. She heard Sandra's almost tearful appeals and Edge's cruel rejection, and then he was beside her, walking carelessly through to the foyer, and when she stole a glance in his direction he seemed totally indifferent to what had just occurred. She shivered. If ever any man spoke to her as Edge had just spoken to Sandra March she felt she would want to curl up and die. And yet Sandra was married. Didn't her husband mean anything to her?

The bellboy willingly carried Sophie's suitcase out to where Edge's car was parked, and Sophie realized why when Edge handed him a five-dollar bill. She wondered whether she should have tipped the boy, but then forgot about it in the other interests of the moment.

Dusk had fallen while they were having their drinks in the bar and now the coolness of evening had a velvety warmth about it. Even the traffic in the busy street seemed to have ebbed somewhat, although there seemed no lessening in the crowds of people thronging into the shops where silver and wood-carvings, Indian silks and Chinese jewellery attracted attention.

Edge's car was an enormous Mercedes station wagon, sleek and powerful, despite its covering film of dust. He unlocked the passenger side door, threw her case inside on to the back seat, and then indicated that she should get in. Sophie did so willingly. She would be glad to get away from the hotel and all the pitfalls it represented. Edge slammed the door behind her and then walked round the bonnet to climb in beside her. He held on to the roof of the vehicle as he got in, sliding into his seat with lithe, supple movements. He pressed the keys into the ignition, but before starting the motor he said:

"You don't have to act as if I were some kind of monster, you know. I assure you, Sandra is perfectly capable of taking care of herself."

Sophie's cheeks flamed and she was glad of the shadows in the car to hide them. "I don't know what you're talking about –"

"Oh yes, you do." He adjusted his clothes more comfortably. "I do have some small knowledge of your sex, and I'm quite aware that you feel a certain amount of sympathy for her."

"It's nothing to do with me."

"I agree. It's not. Nevertheless, save your sympathies for someone who deserves it!"

He flicked the ignition then and the powerful engine roared to life. He turned the wheel with smooth expertise and the large vehicle moved smoothly out of the parking area and into the stream of traffic.

Now Sophie could hear the rhythmic beat of a steel

33

band playing somewhere close at hand, and the pulsating sound caused a sudden and uncontrollable surge of anticipation to run through her body. There was something wholly primitive about that drumming, a wild and stirring penetration of the depths of her consciousness arousing a desire to keep time with the music. She was used to modern music at home, used to moving to the thrumming of electric guitars, but this was different. This was the real thing played by people with generations of African culture behind them. She turned her gaze in Edge St. Vincente's direction, but he seemed totally unaffected by the sounds that came clearly even over the roar of the traffic. No doubt he had heard it all many times before and it was no novelty to him. But to Sophie it was all new and exciting and for a few moments she forgot that she was the interloper here and sighed in pure enjoyment.

The sound drew Edge's attention. "You're tired?" he asked.

Sophie shook her head. "No." She lifted her shoulders and let them fall expressively. "Isn't that music marvellous?"

Edge's lips twisted slightly. "I wonder if you'll be saying that in a few weeks' time."

"Why?" Sophie frowned.

"It's Carnival in three weeks. You'll hear so much pan you'll wish it had never been invented."

"Pan?"

"Sure. That's the common name for the steel bands. You know the instruments were fashioned out of empty oil drums, don't you? Steel pans?"

"Oh, I see." Sophie was interested. "It's fascinating, isn't it?"

34

"That rather depends on what you find fascinating," remarked Edge dryly. "I gather you like that kind of music."

"I like all kinds of music," retorted Sophie defensively. "Don't you?"

Edge shrugged. "I've no doubt you'll have more in common with my son in that respect," he returned, rather sardonically, and Sophie stiffened. His son! Eve hadn't mentioned that Edge had a son!

And then, unwillingly, she recalled something Sandra March had said and which at the time had made no impression on her. She had asked whether – Piers – knew he had a cousin! Of course. She ought to have realized. If he was Eve's cousin, he had to be Edge's son.

She swallowed hard. "Piers?" she managed, rather chokily.

"Yes." Edge looked her way for a moment. "How old did you say you were?"

"I – I'm twenty – five." She felt a wave of sweat break out on her forehead. She had almost said twenty-two!

"Twenty-five," echoed Edge, shaking his head, "You don't look it."

"Thank you for the compliment." She was trying to sound flip, but couldn't. "H – how old is Piers?"

"Didn't my father tell you?"

"He – he may have done. I – I've forgotten." That was reasonable, wasn't it?

"He's seventeen."

"Oh, I see." Sophie bent her head. Seventeen! Only five years younger than she was. So how old did that make this man who was Eve's uncle? And why was she interested anyway?

Edge swung the car out of the bright lights of the main streets into a shadowy suburb where palm trees looked exotic in the glare of the headlights. They were gradually climbing higher and higher out of the town into the hills around, and glancing back Sophie could see the fairyland of lights spreading out below them. She felt an unwelcome twinge of apprehension. Down in the town she had still felt in a sense in command of her own destiny, capable of escaping back to England and denouncing her position if things got too difficult. But no longer. She was here, she was committed to the role she had agreed to play, and she knew instinctively that Edge St. Vincente would brook no uncertainty on her part. He was not the kind of man to play games with, and if ever he found out that she had been deceiving them . . .

The coolness of the breeze through the opened windows of the car had a sea-salt tang about it now. Sophie guessed they were near the sea, but apart from a pale sheen in the moonlight, she could discern nothing. In spite of the difficulties of her position, she found herself eager to see the coastline in daylight. Everything she had seen so far on the island had been almost larger than life in colour and exuberance, and she was convinced the white coral beaches and green surf would be no less exciting. If only she could just think of these things and stop worrying . . .

The silence between them stretched and Sophie felt it was up to her to make some effort to break it. Trying to sound casual, she said: "Tell me about – Pointe St. Vincente. Is – is that the name of your father's house?" Belatedly, she realized that she should have said *my grandfather's* house, but it was too late to do anything about it now.

Happily, however, Edge seemed not to have observed any slip. "No," he replied. "Pointe St. Vincente is the name of the peninsula where the house is situated. The house has no name, except perhaps that it's known locally as the St. Vincente house."

"It – it sounds wonderful!"

"Does it?" Edge's lips twisted. "I shouldn't have thought it would have appealed to you."

"Why?" Sophie was taken aback.

"Surely it's obvious. You must have known of our existence for twenty years, but you've never made any effort before now to contact us."

Sophie flushed. "I – I understood my – my grandfather refused to have anything to do with – with my father."

"So he did. But he would have welcomed some word from you. You are his granddaughter, after all. The innocent party in the affair."

Sophie moved awkwardly. "I – we never talked about it."

"Didn't you?" Edge's lean hands tightened on the wheel as the road swung sharply round a hairpin bend. "I find that hard to believe."

"You don't understand." Sophie warmed to her subject. She had heard Eve's side of the story and could appreciate her dilemma. "My father never got over my mother's death. He – he had loved her very much. He was unable to forget that I was the unwitting cause of her dying. I – I don't say he blamed me exactly, but I must have constantly reminded him. I – well, don't you see? I couldn't have contacted my grandfather in the circumstances. It would have seemed – disloyal."

Edge considered this. "I can see what you're trying to

say," he remarked. "I don't say I agree with it."

"Well, my – my grandfather wasn't an innocent spectator in this affair, was he? I mean, he was responsible for the rift in the first place."

"Maybe so. I can remember he was pretty cut up about it himself. Jennifer had always been the apple of his eye. It was a great shock to him when she chose to ignore everything he had done for her – everything he hoped to do for her – in favour of a penniless engineer!"

"He – my father that is, wasn't penniless!"

"Compared to the wealth my father controls, he was."

"I suppose he would have had her make a marriage of expediency?"

"If, by expediency, you mean he wanted her to marry someone more suitable, then yes –"

"Expediency has other meanings," Sophie broke in, unable to help herself. "It also means more politic than just!"

"Howard Fleming would have made her happy."

"How can you say that?" Sophie was stung by the coolness of his tone. "She obviously didn't love this – this Howard Fleming or she wouldn't have run away with James Hollister!"

Edge's eyes narrowed and as he looked at her she saw the thickness of long black lashes. "James Hollister?" he repeated. "That's a curious way to speak of one's own father."

Sophie knew she had to bluff it out. "Why?" she challenged him. "My father's name was James Hollister, wasn't it?"

Edge returned his attention to the tortuous bends in the road. "If you say so," he commented quietly, and Sophie

38

wondered rather desperately whether she was imagining the note of scepticism in his voice. Surely he must believe she was who she said she was. He couldn't have brought her here otherwise, could he?

Changing the subject entirely, she said: "How much further is it to Pointe St. Vincente?" determinedly forcing herself not to stammer.

Edge flicked back his cuff and consulted the gold watch on his wrist. "About another fifteen minutes," he replied, and Sophie sank more deeply down into her seat, her fingers curving tightly about the soft leather upholstery. Soon they would be there and she had to prepare herself for the ordeal to come.

The moon had risen by the time they reached the curving drive which led down to the St. Vincente house. In its pale glow, Sophie could see tree-clad slopes, leading down to a natural harbour below the house where shadowy buildings indicated boathouses. But the house itself was what held her spellbound, the floodlit gardens giving its white-painted façade unnatural colour. It was a split-level dwelling, seemingly welded into the hillside itself with shallow stone steps leading down between pergolas laden with bougainvillea and other climbing plants to a stone-paved area for cars. The various sections of the building spread themselves comfortably in all directions with a complete disregard for balance or design, and yet for all that it was one of the most beautiful buildings Sophie had ever seen.

Edge brought the Mercedes to a smooth halt in the paved courtyard which was slightly to the side of the house, and as Sophie thrust open her door and climbed out she heard the unmistakable hiss and thunder of the ocean on the rocks below. She thought it would be very easy for someone to get an inflated opinion of themselves in such surroundings, but Edge St. Vincente seemed to take it all for granted.

He got out of the car too, and as he reached into the back for her suitcase someone came hurrying down the steps towards them. As the newcomer drew nearer, Sophie saw it was a black-skinned manservant dressed immaculately in dark trousers and a white jacket and he grinned at Edge with easy familiarity.

"Your pa's getting mighty anxious about you, Mr. Edge," he said, taking the suitcase from his master's hand automatically. His gaze flicked to Sophie. "Is this here Miss Jennifer's daughter?"

Edge's lips twitched. "That's right, Joseph. This is – Miss Eve Hollister."

Joseph nodded warmly in Sophie's direction. "Mr. Brandt, he's gonna be sure glad to see you, Miss Eve. Ain't been no young women around the St. Vincente house in many a long day!"

Sophie looked up at Edge, standing so indolently beside her. He had hooked his thumbs into the belt of his pants and was regarding Joseph with lazy resignation. She thought that everything he did had an unconscious grace about it. He moved lithely, lazily even; and yet she could sense the latent strength that lay just below the surface, the sinuous power that had an almost sensual tangibility. It was this quality he possessed which disturbed her so. She was consciously aware of him, and the knowledge troubled her somewhat.

Joseph became aware that he was delaying them and drew back to allow Edge to urge Sophie up the steps to the house. As they walked she could hear the sound of the crickets like a steady hum above the sound of the sea, and she had to squash the feeling of intense excitement that seemed to be welling up inside her and choking her throat.

When they reached the top of the steps and she stopped at the entrance to the house, Edge bumped into her and for a moment his hand was on her arm, supporting her, as he apologized.

"It – it was my fault," said Sophie jerkily, pulling herself away from him. She was unnecessarily abrupt, but for a moment his flesh had burned hers and she couldn't help but be aware of it. She had felt the hardness of his lean body, her arms had brushed against the soft silk of his shirt beneath which the muscles of his chest had been disturbingly firm, and she had known an intense, and wholly incomprehensible desire to remain there against him. She wasn't used to experiencing feelings like this, and she chided herself for being stupidly imaginative. Heavens, she was supposed to be his niece! What would he have thought of her if he had been able to read her thoughts just then?

Edge led the way through a mesh door into a cool tiled hall. The hall appeared to run from front to back of the building with several other passages leading from it, while a curved wrought iron staircase led to the upper floors. A tall stand supported a vase of gorgeously coloured lilies, their fleshy stamens protruding in a totally alien fashion. The hall was illuminated by a copper-based lamp that had a painted Chinese shade.

Sophie looked about her a trifle bemusedly. There was so much colour and beauty to absorb, but Edge was urging her forward, taking her across the hall and up a short

41

flight of stairs to halt before a dark blue panelled door.

"This is my father's study," he remarked, in explanation, and then pressed the handle and swung open the door.

Sophie stepped forward into a comfortably furnished room, with skin rugs on the floor and a desk dominating the central area. She saw walls lined with leather volumes, filing cabinets, and a low couch, and a small table on which stood a couple of filing baskets and a typewriter. Clearly it was from here that Brandt St. Vincente conducted the affairs of the estate.

But then a man rose from behind the desk to greet her; and all further impressions of the room ceased as the man commanded her whole attention.

Brandt St. Vincente was nothing like she had imagined. After Eve's appeals to her to come here to Trinidad to assuage the needs of an old man, Sophie had expected him to be in his seventies, frail and ill, living every day without really knowing how much time he had left.

The real man was totally different. Like his son, he was years younger than she had expected, in his early sixties, she estimated. And what was more, he was a man in his prime, tall and vigorous, more heavily built than his son but very much like him, with thick hair that was greying now, and strong handsome features.

He came round his desk to greet her, holding out both hands, and she put hers into them automatically, unable to deny the welcome he was showing her.

"So you're Eve!" he exclaimed, shaking his head. "My Jennifer's girl! I can hardly believe it."

"Why?" The word was scarcely more than a whisper, but it was all Sophie could think to say.

Brandt squeezed her hands tightly. "It's been so long,"

he said, rather emotionally. But then he seemed to gather his composure again, and he went on: "I don't suppose you knew anything about your mother."

"Not a lot," admitted Sophie, nervously. "She – er – my father seldom spoke of her. It – it was too painful for him."

At the mention of James Hollister's name, Brandt's face changed. His lips tightened perceptibly and his brown eyes lost some of their warmth.

"I think it would be as well if we forgot the past and concentrated on the present, don't you? I mean, it's obvious that there are things which if said would be painful to both of us. It's no use resurrecting past grievances. And we've both had our share of grief, believe me. I suggest we begin afresh, learn to know one another without the distorting influences that were created by other people so many years ago."

Sophie nodded slowly. "I – I'm willing," she murmured, looking down at her hands clasped in his.

"Good! Good!" Brandt's expression softened again. "You've no idea how happy you've made me. I've so looked forward to your coming here, to meeting you. We're your family now, this is where you belong. Oh, I know you've got your career, but surely the family should come first, in spite of everything!"

Sophie stared at him. She didn't quite know how to answer him. But to her relief, she didn't have to.

"Relax!" he exclaimed. "Don't look so nervous! We won't bite, I promise you. On the contrary, it will be delightful to have a young woman about the place again."

Sophie glanced behind her. All the while his father had been speaking Edge had been standing silently near the door, watching them, a lazy smile playing about his lips. But now he stepped forward and said: "Joseph said practically the same thing. If I'd know you were both so eager for feminine company . . ."

His voice trailed away insinuatively and Brandt looked impatiently at his son. "Don't be sarcastic, Edge. If this is any example of the welcome you've given your niece, I'm not surprised she looks nervous!"

Edge looked speculatively at Sophie. "Well, perhaps we're not what she expected either."

"What do you mean?" Brandt glared at him.

Edge shrugged. "Oh, nothing." He looked away from Sophie and drew his cigar case out of his pocket. "I think I'll go and change for dinner. I feel rather – hot and uncomfortable." His eyes flickered over Sophie again. "Perhaps – my niece would like to shower and change, too."

Brandt released Sophie's hands apologetically and went to pull a long velvet cord hanging near a screened fireplace. "Of course, of course," he exclaimed. "In the excitement of meeting you, my dear, I'm forgetting common courtesy. Of course, you must be tired and hungry. I'll have Violet show you to your room and we'll dine in – say –" he glanced at his wrist watch, "– say – thirty minutes? Do you think that will be long enough for you to get ready?"

"Of – of course." Sophie cupped her hands together. "I – I'd just like to say I'm – I'm very happy to be here."

Edge, a cigar between his teeth, walked to the door. "Oh, well said," he remarked mockingly, and Sophie's hands clenched into fists.

"Ignore your uncle," advised Brandt, giving his son a

44

reproving glance. "Edge has a very cynical mind."

Edge swung open the door and leant against the jamb for a moment. "You always said we had a lot in common, Brandt," he remarked lazily, and the door closed behind him with a definite click.

After he had gone the room seemed suddenly empty. Sophie looked awkwardly at Eve's grandfather. "You – you have a beautiful house," she murmured. "I – I'm longing to see it in daylight."

"Indeed, yes." Brandt seemed to relax and came towards her again smiling down into her eyes. "I'm sure you're going to be happy here, Eve. If you're not, it won't be through the fault of not trying on my part. I intend to make your stay so enjoyable that you won't want to leave us again. We have so much here to interest you." He spread and encompassing hand. "Swimming; sailing; skin-diving, if you're adventurous enough. Edge and Piers would teach you. They spend hours out in the boat. Then, of course, the island itself is a veritable paradise for nature-lovers. We have so many different species of birds. We must take you to the Caroni bird sanctuary to see the scarlet ibis. I don't suppose you've seen it in its natural habitat." He sighed. "You see, my dear, already I'm anticipating the weeks ahead with a great deal of satisfaction."

Sophie was saved the need of responding to this small speech by a knock at the door. At Brandt's bidding a black-skinned servant appeared, and he smiled.

"Ah, Violet," he said, putting an arm round Sophie. "Eve, my dear, allow me to introduce you to our treasure, Violet." The black woman chuckled and he went on: "She smoothes all our lives without us really appreciating

45

it, don't you, Violet?"

"If you say so, Mr. Brandt." Violet's dark luminous eyes shifted to the girl at his side. "How do you do, Miss Eve. I'm pleased to meet you."

"Hello, Violet." Sophie managed a smile.

"Will you show Miss Eve to her room, Violet?" added Brandt, propelling Sophie forward. "Then we'll have dinner in half an hour."

"Yes, sir, Mr. Brandt." Violet stepped back into the corridor behind her. "Will you follow me, miss?"

After receiving another encouraging smile from Eve's grandfather, Sophie accompanied Violet back along the passage to the hall. They crossed to the wrought iron staircase and had just begun to climb when a young man came in through the mesh door and saw them. He was tall and very lean, his bony body accentuated by close-fitting hipster jeans and a collarless sweat shirt. When he saw them he looked up in surprise, his gaze moving over Sophie as Edge's had done. Sophie guessed that this must be Piers, but he was not as dark as his father and his hair was longer. However, he had lazily attractive features, less aggressively masculine than his father's.

"Well, well," he commented, moving to the foot of the stairs. "You must be Eve, am I right?"

Sophie saw that Violet had halted ahead of her and was obviously waiting for her to respond to Piers' informal introduction. She nodded. "Yes, I'm – Eve. And you, of course, are Piers."

"I do have that dubious distinction." Piers laughed. "Aren't you coming down to say hello to your long-lost cousin?"

Violet leaned over the balustrade. "Mr. Brandt said

46

dinner was to be served in half an hour, Mr. Piers. Miss Eve needs time to wash and tidy herself before then."

Piers made a face. "Family dinner," he mocked. Then: "And have you met our *family*, Eve?"

Sophie hesitated. "All except Great-aunt Rosalind, I believe."

"Rosa?" Piers' lips twitched. "Ah, well, that's a treat in store."

"Mr. Piers!" Violet sounded reproving.

"I know, I know. I shouldn't speak disrespectfully of my elders, but really . . . Don't take too much notice of what she says, will you, Eve?"

Sophie was saved from replying by Violet's expressive snort and when the servant continued on up the winding staircase, Sophie followed her without looking back.

But a smile was touching her lips, too. She liked Piers. He was nice and – uncomplicated. She thought she could understand him. But she'd never understand his father; never in a million years . . .

CHAPTER THREE

SOPHIE'S room was situated on the curving side of the house, and when she stepped out on to her balcony next morning, she almost caught her breath at the beauty of the view which awaited her.

Below the shallow steps leading down to the paved courtyard which she and Edge had climbed the night below, the thickly foliaged garden fell away sharply to disappear at the edge of what appeared to be a precipitous drop to the sea below. She knew there were boathouses down there however, and guessed there was some means of descending to the rocks beneath. But the sea itself was enchanting – a bewitching translucent shade of turquoise, glittering and sparkling in the strengthening rays of the sun. Already it was very warm, and Sophie, who had slept restlessly, longed to shed her clothes and plunge into those sun-warmed depths.

But as yet she didn't know the routine of the household and while she longed to explore she would have to wait until she was invited to do so. So she contented herself with showering in the exquisitely appointed bathroom which adjoined her bedroom and thought rather seriously of the difficult situation Eve had thrust her into.

It had become increasingly obvious that Eve's reasons for concealing her relatives' real ages from her had been a deliberate ploy to get her here, for the other girl must have known perfectly well that Sophie would never have agreed unless she had been able to appeal to the sympathetic side of her nature. Sophie supposed she ought to be furious really, but the circumstances were such that she could not deny the surge of pure excitement that filled her at the thought of the weeks ahead.

All the same, she thought as she sobered, her position here was not going to be any sinecure, and there was still the disturbing problem of why Eve had chosen to pretend to her that her grandfather had not known of her occupation when in fact he did. Unless she had imagined, probably with good reason, that Sophie herself would have seen this as one more reason why she should not take the risk and come here. After all, what did she know of that side of Eve's life? Very little!

But she refused to worry about that now. This was her first day in Trinidad and she intended to enjoy it, if she could.

Wrapping one of the huge bath-towels sarong-wise round her slender body, she walked back into her bedroom. This was a beautiful room, too, with cream and apricot curtains, and an embossed cream bedcover. The fine linen sheets were cream, too, while there were fleecy rugs of dark tan and apricot wool on the cool terrazzo-tiled floor.

While she was at dinner the previous evening, her suitcase had been unpacked and its contents hung away in the long cupboards which were fitted against one wall, but now she swung open one of the louvre doors and looked inside thoughtfully.

She had brought plenty of uncrushable summer dresses, some jeans and tops, and one rather special gown for evenings. But now she chose a short white pleated skirt, edged with navy, and a boat-necked, sleeveless cotton top, also in navy, which made her skin look rather pale. Still, she thought rather wryly, treading into cork-heeled sandals, providing she was allowed to stay here long enough, that was a condition she could easily change.

Thinking of remaining here brought thoughts of dinner the previous evening. It had been a curiously unreal evening altogether, with Edge presiding sardonically at one end of the long polished table, and his father presiding at the other. The table had been set in a kind of glass conservatory with candelabra providing the only illumination, and Sophie thought it had been as much that as her imagination which had caused her to feel that Edge had a disturbingly satanic look when those tawny eyes were turned in her direction.

Brandt St. Vincente had been kind, introducing her to his sister Rosalind with obvious pride. But Sophie couldn't relax with him either. She was deceiving him, she was an interloper here, and she couldn't help but be aware of it.

But she had understood what Piers meant about his great-aunt. She must have once been very beautiful, but now she was merely a pale shadow of her former self, living a little in the past, nervous and absent-minded, appearing much older than her strong, forceful brother. It struck Sophie that perhaps Eve's mother had been right to escape while she could, and then she chided herself for such thoughts. But perhaps the men of this family had that effect on their women, and Jennifer must have known that as well as anyone.

Only Piers had seemed, to Sophie, someone with whom she could be herself, or as near herself as it was possible to be when one was supposed to be someone else. He had talked naturally with her asking questions about London and England, and these she could answer truthfully and without restraint. But all the while she had been conscious of his father watching them, and she had been glad when after dinner Edge had disappeared about his own pursuits. No one asked where he was going and he had volunteered no information, but the atmosphere was distinctly different after he had gone.

She was brushing her hair when the sound of voices and someone whistling down in the courtyard drifted through the open french doors. Putting down her brush, she quickly crossed the room and looked rather surreptitiously over her balcony rail. But she need not have worried. No one was taking any notice of her. On the contrary, Edge and Piers, and the manservant Joseph, were far too concerned with what they were doing to pay any attention to a balcony on the first floor.

They were crossing the courtyard together carrying masks and flippers and oxygen cylinders, clearly intent on the sport ahead. Sophie couldn't help envying them. It was exactly what she would have liked to have done. She felt sure that the waters around Pointe St. Vincente positively teemed with fish and other marine life.

The men, all dressed casually in shorts and tank tops, disappeared down a path which Sophie had not previously noticed but which she now saw led to the edge of the cliff. She guessed it led to the steps down to the cove below.

Turning back into the room behind her, she wondered why she suddenly felt so deflated. If Edge and Piers were to be away for the day she should feel relieved, but she didn't. Perhaps it was because she had looked forward to seeing Piers again, she thought, and now it looked as though she was going to be disappointed.

It was a little after eight when she left her room and went along the tiled corridor which led to a short flight of stairs which in turn led down to the main gallery from where the circular staircase descended to the hall. In the hall, she encountered one of the young maids and asked her where she was supposed to have breakfast.

"You want breakfast downstairs, miss?" asked the girl in her sing-song voice.

Sophie shrugged. "Isn't that the usual practice?"

The girl moved her head from side to side. "Sometimes, sometimes not. Mr. Edge, sometimes he has breakfast early, very early, and other times he has breakfast in bed."

"Oh – oh, I see." Sophie felt herself colouring slightly. "Well – er – I don't mind really. Whichever is most convenient."

The girl was eyeing her rather strangely now and Sophie realized she was expected to make a decision herself, not to leave it to this girl. Obviously her attitude was not the accepted one, but she wasn't used to giving orders.

However, to her relief, at that moment Violet appeared, her black face showing some concern as she saw the other servant's indolent stance.

"What is wrong, Miss Eve?" she asked sharply. "This girl has been insolent? Liza, get back to the kitchen. I will deal with you later –"

"No, really, I –" Sophie sighed. "There's been no trouble, Violet. I simply didn't understand where I was expected to have breakfast."

"Ah!" Violet nodded, but the flick of her fingers sent the girl Liza scurrying back to the kitchen. "You are hungry, yes?" she nodded vigorously.

52

"A little," admitted Sophie, conscious of a slightly hollow feeling in the region of her ribcage.

"Good! Good! Come this way."

Violet showed her into a sun-filled room to the right of the hall which opened on to a terrace overlooking the luxuriant garden at the front of the house. Compared to Brandt St. Vincente's study and the lounge they had used the night before after dinner, this was a comparatively small room with a glass-topped circular table set by the long french doors which stood wide, and tall cabinets filled with china and glass.

"Go and sit on the terrace and I will bring your breakfast in five minutes," promised Violet with a smile, and Sophie nodded her thanks. "This is the morning room," she went on. "Mr. Brandt usually lunches in here, as no doubt you'll soon discover for yourself."

"Thank you, Violet. I hope I'm not causing any trouble."

Violet's eyes warmed perceptibly. "Heavens, no, Miss Eve. It's a pleasure to have you here. Why, I nursed your mother when she was no more than a few minutes old, and I always used to look forward to the day when I'd be nursing her baby, too." She shook her head a trifle sadly. "As if I'd find looking after her daughter any trouble, miss!"

Sophie felt terrible. Why, oh, why had Violet had to say that? Until then she had felt at ease, but now the old familiar feeling of deceit was creeping over her again. Walking quickly to the windows she changed the subject abruptly by saying:

"Er – isn't this a wonderful view? I don't think I've ever seen anywhere more beautiful."

53

Violet sniffed. "I must see about your breakfast, miss," she said firmly, and went out of the room.

Sophie turned as she left and felt an awful sense of depression. She was wishing more and more that she had not allowed Eve to persuade her to come here, her earlier spasm of excitement doused by the ordinary events of the day. But she would have to stick it out now that she was here, and the sooner she stopped reproaching herself for weakening the easier it would be. She must try to think of herself as acting a part, the part of Eve Hollister, and at no time must she allow her own personal feelings to intrude.

Violet provided her with an English breakfast and to her surprise Sophie found herself enjoying it. She was finishing her third cup of delicious Havana coffee when the door opened and Eve's grandfather appeared.

"Good morning, Eve," he said, with evident warmth, coming towards her to press one of her hands affectionately. "It's good to see you here at my table. It's where you belong. Now, tell me: how did you sleep?"

"Very well, thank you – er – Grandfather."

"You find that difficult to say, don't you?" he asked, and when she looked blank, he explained: "Grandfather! You find it difficult to think of me as your grandfather?"

Sophie didn't know how to reply. "Why – er – not really –" she began, but he was not convinced.

"I think you do," he insisted. "Very well then. You shall call me Brandt as Piers does. How does that appeal to you?"

Sophie stared at him, the tip of her tongue just appearing between her teeth. "I – if that's all right with you," she murmured awkwardly, wondering what Eve would have said in the same circumstances.

"Good, good." Brandt seemed satisfied with this. "Maybe in time we'll find some more intimate form of address, but for the moment that will do."

Sophie gave what she hoped was an agreeable smile and he went on: "Have you finished your breakfast?"

She nodded. "I'm afraid so. It was marvellous. I can see I shall put on weight while I'm here."

"Then I thought this morning we might go and take a look at the estate, if you're interested."

"The estate," echoed Sophie softly, getting to her feet. "Oh yes, I'd love to. But don't you want any breakfast?"

"I have what I want brought up to me at seven-thirty every morning," Brandt informed her, thrusting his hands into the pockets of his well-fitting beige riding breeches, and Sophie thought how well that rigid statement fitted in with what she had already learned about him. He was a powerful, dominant man, strict with himself as well as others, spurning the softer existence he might have had in favour of the self-discipline he had always practised.

Now he straightened his back and asked if she was ready to leave at once.

"Why, yes, I suppose I am." Sophie glanced round at the dirty dishes. "Do you think – I mean, oughtn't I to carry these things to the kitchen?"

Brandt frowned. "Of course not. One of the maids will deal with that. That's their job." His expression softened. "You must get used to allowing other people to do things for you. I don't suppose you've had much waiting on in the past."

"No." Sophie shook her head. "Will I need a cardigan or anything?"

"I shouldn't think so." Brandt himself was wearing no jacket over his short-sleeved cream shirt. "We'll go in the station wagon. Do you ride, by the way?"

"I'm afraid not." Sophie answered automatically, and then felt her nerves tensing. Eve *could* ride. She had learned at the girls' school her father had sent her to. She remembered her telling her that at some distant time in the past. Still, she calmed herself, Brand couldn't know that or he wouldn't have asked, would he?

"Then that's something else we must teach you." His words cut across her thoughts, calming her. He put a casual arm across her shoulders. "Come along, let's go. I'm looking forward to showing you more of our domain."

The St. Vincente estate was extensive, as Sophie had guessed it would be. Much of the inland area was cultivated by cocoa plantations, the trees still bearing the machete scars of the recent harvest. Brandt said it had been a good harvest, but he went on to explain that although the plantations provided employment for many of his people, his main source of income came from the other end of the island, form the oil concessions which could bring such unlimited wealth and which had become the mainstay of the island's economy.

But to Sophie, the tall cocoa trees with their downward sweeping leathery leaves represented something real and fundamental, and she was glad she did not have to see the oil derricks and their accompanying mess of machinery.

She was fascinated to see bananas growing in their natural state, hanging in bunches from the trees that could

56

provide such appealing avenues of shade. Even sheltered from the sun in the dust-smeared station wagon it was incredibly hot, and she looked forward to their return and the cool shower she intended to indulge in.

All the same, she enjoyed being with Brandt. Like all self-made men he knew his business inside out. He knew the life of a coffee bean from its first inception in the pod to the ultimate refinement of a bar of milk chocolate. He could regale Sophie with the various difficulties faced by a cocoa planter and by the time they returned to the house she felt quite knowledgeable on the subject. She couldn't help but wonder how Edge St. Vincente would react if she started discussing the possible remedies for a fungicidal disease with him.

The only jarring note that she experienced came when they visited one of the villages near the plantation for her to see the drying piles of cocoa beans. The conditions the people lived in appalled Sophie, but when she mentioned this to Brandt he seemed unmoved. It was obvious he saw nothing distressing in the lack of amenities, and did not regard his position as a privileged one.

"You're too squeamish, Eve," he told her as they drove back to the house. "The accommodation is adequate, schools are provided free by the government. If they're overcrowded they have only themselves to blame."

"But there should be some sort of control –" began Sophie, when Brandt shook his head.

"When you start imposing controls on people's liberties it smacks of dictatorship."

"Birth control isn't like that," she protested.

"Here the people accept what God provides and are thankful. Eve, they're happy! Didn't you notice that?
57

You think scrubbed floors and flush toilets make people happy?"

Sophie coloured. "I didn't say that."

"No, but that was what you meant, wasn't it?" Brandt smiled. "I can see we shall have to educate you in other ways, Eve."

It was after noon when they arrived back at the house and Sophie excused herself and went up to her room. It was a relief to shed her clothes and plunge under a cold shower and afterwards she stretched on her bed to relax. The heat and the tension had tired her and she was almost asleep when there was a knock at her door and a maid entered carrying a tray on which stood a small jug of iced chocolate and some small biscuits.

Sophie levered herself up on one arm, automatically holding the towel closer about her. "Oh, thank you," she said, smiling. "Just put it on the table there."

The maid did as she was asked and as she straightened Sophie saw she was the girl she had spoken to that morning. "Mr. Brandt said to tell you that lunch is at two, Miss Eve. He thought you might like this to fill the gap."

"Thank you." Sophie tried to get the girl to smile in return, but she merely nodded her head and left her.

After she had gone, Sophie poured herself some of the sweet-smelling liquid and after tasting it found she liked it. She ate one of the small biscuits and then relaxed again. Her spirits were rising and she found a smile touching her lips. After all, the morning had been incredibly easy really, and once she was accepted here it must get easier. Perhaps Eve was not such a menace as she had thought . . .

She had lunch with Brandt and Rosa on the terrace. As

58

there was still no sign of Edge or Piers she commented upon it, and Brandt explained.

"We own a small charter company out of Port of Spain," he said. "A couple of yachts, a schooner, motor launches, that sort of thing. Yesterday an American couple wanted to hire a yacht, but unfortunately the skipper was ill and a rather inexperienced crewman took them out. He ran the craft on to a point some distance round the island near the Dragon's Mouth."

"The Dragon's Mouth?" Sophie didn't understand.

"It's part of the narrow channel of water which divides Trinidad from the Venezuelan mainland," explained Brandt patiently.

"I see. Was anyone hurt?"

"Not seriously, I don't think. A few cuts and bruises, but that's all. They were lucky. But the yacht's holed and needs towing back to Port of Spain for repair. That's what Edge and Piers are doing."

"Oh." Sophie applied herself to the shellfish on her plate. "Is – is that part of – my uncle's duties?"

"Edge?" Brandt shrugged, and reached into his pocket for one of the fat cigars he seemed to enjoy between courses. "I suppose you could say that, although actually the plantation is his pigeon. In fact I suppose you could call him a business manager for all the St. Vincente companies. That's his – what would you call it? – profession, accountancy. I guess he doesn't actually do any figure work now, except maybe to check on somebody else, but no one gets away with anything when he's around."

Sophie felt a twinge of unease. "I can believe that," she murmured with feeling.

Brandt smiled. "Hey, do I detect a note of cynicism in

your voice, Eve?" he chided gently. "You mustn't let him rub you up the wrong way, you know."

Rosa St. Vincente wiped her mouth delicately on her table napkin. "You couldn't expect to bring Jennifer's daughter here without Edge showing some reaction," she said, in her rather high-pitched voice.

Brandt clicked his tongue. "Couldn't I? And why not? You're surely not trying to imply that Edge is jealous!"

Rosa shook her head. "Oh, no. Edge has too generous a nature to be jealous."

"Then what do you mean?"

Sophie sensed the growing impatience behind Brandt's controlled civility.

"I mean Howard, of course."

"Oh!" Brandt chewed the end of his unlit cigar broodingly. "And why should Eve's coming here affect Howard? That's past history, Rosa."

"He's never married."

"That means absolutely nothing."

"I think he still thinks of Jennifer."

Brandt's lips tightened. "You live in the past, Rosa," he stated shortly.

"Do I?" His sister raised a chiffon handkerchief to her lips. "Perhaps I do." She shrugged her bony shoulders. "Nevertheless, everyone knows Howard was heartbroken when Jennifer ran away with – with –"

"That will do, Rosa!" Brandt was abrupt now. "Eve, you haven't touched your wine. Drink up. It will do you good."

Sophie picked up her wine glass obediently and then put it down again. If she wasn't careful she would be allowing Brandt to dictate to her as he did to the other members of his family. Except Edge, taunted a small voice, but she ignored it.

When lunch was over Rosa excused herself and although Brandt did not immediately rise from the table Sophie could tell he had other things than his new-found granddaughter on his mind.

"Do you mind if I go to my room?" she asked tentatively, pushing back her chair, and saw his face clear.

"No. No, of course not, my dear. I have some work to do myself, and it's too hot for you to be outside. I suggest we meet on the terrace for afternoon tea about five o'clock."

"All right."

Sophie smiled and left him, making her way to her room without difficulty. She was beginning to understand a little of the layout of the house, and while she would have liked to have explored every room she was content to wait until the opportunity presented itself.

But in her room she was restless, and although she had been tired earlier, sleep would not now come. Rosa St. Vincente's words had affected her strongly and she found herself speculating about the unknown Howard. She had realized that this must be the Howard Fleming that Edge had spoken about in the car coming from Port of Spain, and she wondered whether indeed Jennifer's precipitous elopement had upset him as much as Rosa seemed to think. He would be a man several years older than Edge, of course, but that would still only mean that he was somewhere in his early forties. A man in his prime, some might say, so why hadn't he married?

Towards late afternoon she heard voices again below her windows and realized that Edge and Piers must have returned. The knowledge gave her a feeling of stimulation far in advance of its importance and she felt impatient with herself for reacting so.

At five o'clock she put on an orange tunic-styled dress and went down to the terrace for afternoon tea. The morning room was deserted, but when she stepped out on to the tiled area beyond she found Piers sprawled in a basketwork lounger.

"Well, hi!" he exclaimed, scrambling in an ungainly fashion to his feet. "You look nice and cool. What have you been doing with yourself all day?"

Sophie seated herself in a cane chair and shrugged. "This and that. I went out with – with my grandfather this morning, but this afternoon I've been resting."

"Resting?" Piers was aghast. "At your age? Haven't you been in the sea?"

"No." Sophie shook her head. "Perhaps tomorrow –"

"Tomorrow nothing!" Piers interrupted. "Go get your swimsuit on and we'll go down now."

"Go down?" echoed Sophie faintly.

"Sure! To swim! You'd like that, wouldn't you? And it's great at this time of day when the water's really warm."

Sophie didn't know what to say. "But I'm supposed to be having tea with Brandt."

"Oh, he won't mind. Besides, you'll be back before you know where you are." He hooked his thumbs into the waistband of his shorts and grinned at her. "Well, go on. Get ready!"

"I don't know if I should ..." began Sophie uncomfortably.

"Nonsense! You know you're dying to get in the water.

62

Hell, you can't spend another night in Trinidad without experiencing what it's like to swim here. Honestly, you'll love it."

"I'm sure I would, but –"

"But nothing!" Piers raised his eyebrows impatiently. "My, you take some persuading!"

Sophie came to a decision. She got nervously to her feet. "Well, if you're sure it will be all right –"

"Of course I'm sure. I shouldn't have asked you otherwise, would I?"

"I suppose not." Sophie bit her lower lip. "All right. Give me five minutes."

In her room she dragged the white bikini which the sales girl in the Regent Street store had assured her everyone wore these days out of the drawer and looked at it doubtfully. Then with a shrug she began to strip off her clothes.

Once on the bikini looked even more diminuative, and she wondered why she had allowed anyone to persuade her that such a garment was adequate covering. There seemed such a length of pale arms and legs, while she had never before bared her midriff to the sun.

But it was too late to regret her impulsive buying now and she could only be thankful that she had also bought a green and white striped towelling jacket to wear over it.

She went back downstairs again with some misgivings, tying the belt of the jacket as she went. She was halfway down the wrought iron staircase when Edge St. Vincente came into the hall and saw her.

Immediately, the scarcity of her attire seemed more pronounced and she would have given anything to be able to turn round and rush back upstairs again. But of course she couldn't do that. This man was supposed to be her uncle and any attention he might pay to her was simply the avuncular interest paid by someone in his position to his niece.

So she continued to the bottom and stepped on to the mosaic tiling of the hall in time to see him stretching lazily, his navy tank top separating from his white shorts to reveal a smooth expanse of brown skin. Then his arms dropped to his sides again and the tawny eyes appraised her.

When he didn't say anything, Sophie had to. "I – er – Piers is taking me swimming," she volunteered.

"Is he?" Edge moved his head in assent.

"Yes. I – I haven't been in the water yet."

"No."

He was annoyingly unforthcoming, but he was standing directly in her path and unless she walked right round him she couldn't pass.

"Have – have you had a successful day? Did you manage to recover your boat?" she asked, hoping to distract his probing eyes.

Edge shrugged. "We recovered the yacht, yes. I would hardly call it a successful day exactly. The insurers aren't going to be too happy about paying out for its repair in the circumstances."

"Oh, I see." Sophie half smiled, but receiving no encouragement sobered. "I expect you're tired."

"Not particularly. We slept on the launch this afternoon." At last he stepped aside. "I hear my father took you over the estate this morning."

"Yes, that's right. I found it very interesting."

"Did you?" His expression was a little sardonic now.

64

"Of course, you would. I imagine he told you it's quite a lucrative business."

Sophie was walking past him, but his words halted her. Looking up at him she frowned. "I'm not sure, but I think that sounded rather rude," she said tremulously.

"Did it?" His eyes narrowed. "Perhaps I should have spoken more plainly."

Sophie stared at him searchingly, but his mocking gaze was not to be sustained. Bending her head, she murmured: "Piers will be waiting for me," and received a gesture of dismissal for her pains. But even as she took a step forward, Piers himself appeared from the direction of the morning room, a red and white towel draped over one shoulder.

His expression lightened when he saw Sophie, and he smiled. "You're back! I was beginning to think you'd had second thoughts."

"I'm afraid I'm responsible for detaining her, Piers," drawled Edge, stretching again. "But don't let me detain you any longer, children."

Sophie refused to look at him. Instead, she smiled at Piers and said: "Yes, let's go."

The sun was cooling perceptibly now and there was a faint refreshing breeze to fan their faces as they descended the worn stone steps to the cove below. There was an iron hand-rail for support and Sophie, trying to banish all thoughts of Edge from her mind, wondered whether indeed she might need some support coming up again. It would be quite a climb.

The steps gave on to a concrete jetty where a couple of wooden boathouses revealed a small racing dinghy and a motor launch, no doubt the same launch as they had used earlier. The ropes creaked a little as the boats moved on the swell and there was a delightful smell of salt in the air. The sea was the same translucent colour it had been from above, only now it was possible to see into its depths where dozens of small fish swam among green-shadowed rocks and plant life waved invitingly.

Further along the jetty, a shelf of virtually flat rocks led some way out into the water. Piers quickly shed his shorts and top to reveal brief navy swimming trunks and then sprang agilely across these rocks, looking back to find Sophie still hesitating on the brink.

"Come on," he said. "It's quite safe. You can swim, can't you?"

"Yes," said Sophie doubtfully, unloosening the sash of her towelling jacket. "Is it very deep?"

"Out here?" Piers wrinkled his nose. "Not very. No more than ten feet anyway."

"Ten feet!" Sophie's eyes widened.

Piers put his hands on his hips. "Are you coming or aren't you? For heaven's sake, get that jacket off and come on."

Sophie heaved a sigh and allowed the jacket to fall about her ankles and Piers bowed his head in acknow-ledgement.

"Very nice," he said, as she scrambled across the rocks to his side. "But too pale. Never mind, we'll soon have you as brown as I am."

Sophie doubted it. Piers, like his father, was tanned all over, a deep attractive tan which would probably take years to acquire.

Now Piers walked to the edge of the rocks and looked down speculatively. Then he looked back at Sophie.

"Do you dive?"

"I can do. But I'd rather not," confessed Sophie nervously. "Couldn't I just sort of slide in the first time?"

Piers indicated the sweep of the bay, pointing to a small promontory that rose out of the water. "Apart from that rock, the Pointe, that gives Pointe St. Vincente its name, there's nothing to be afraid of here. There's hardly any swell, and no currents. I'll go in first, and you follow me."

He dived smoothly into the water, emerging to shake his head like an animal might have done. He pushed his hair out of his eyes and then swam back to where Sophie still faltered. "Come on! It's easy. Jump in!"

Sophie hesitated only a moment longer and then gripping her nose tightly she jumped off the rocks and down into the water. The initial coldness made her gasp, but by the time she had emerged again she had realized that in fact it was quite warm. Looking round she saw Piers some distance away and struck out towards him with a lazy crawl, revelling in the feeling of the buoyant water against her heated flesh.

"Well?" said Piers, as she reached him. "It's not so bad, is it?"

"No, it's marvellous!" Sophie trod water, looking about her with eager eyes. "I've never swum much in the sea before. It's always too cold back home."

"I'm not surprised," Piers nodded. "It was jolly cold when I was in England. You'll have to make up for it while you're here."

They swam and played for a while and then Piers, who was wearing a watch, said he thought they ought to go back as it was after six o'clock and Brandt might be getting anxious.

"After six o'clock!" Sophie was horrified. "Gosh, I thought it would be around five-thirty!"

Piers laughed. "It's my stimulating company, Eve. I take that as a compliment."

Sophie laughed too and they swam to the side and scrambled out. Sophie's legs felt curiously weak, however, and she realized the unaccustomed exercise had tired her more than she thought. Piers, noticing her weariness, said: "We'll rest for a while before going up to the house, shall we?"

"Oh, but what about your grandfather?" Sophie blurted before really thinking of what she was saying.

"*My* grandfather!" echoed Piers, in surprise. "He's your grandfather, too."

Sophie flushed. "Yes, I know that. It's just that — well, I guess it takes a little getting used to."

Piers accepted this and after drying his body he put on his clothes again and squatted down beside her on the sun-warmed jetty. "Do you think you're going to like it here?" he asked kindly.

Sophie shrugged. "I — I'm sure I shall."

"So you'll be staying then?"

"Staying?" Sophie was confused.

"Sure. Dad said you wouldn't want to, but Brandt hopes you will."

Sophie thought furiously. So that was the way the land lay! She ought to have guessed that Brandt St. Vincente was not the kind of man to let an opportunity like this escape him. Jennifer had freed herself of his control, but Jennifer's daughter might not find it so easy . . .

Suddenly they were hailed from above and looking up Sophie saw the subject of her thoughts at the top of the steps beckoning to them. Piers got resignedly to his feet.

"Come on," he said. "I gather we've been summoned to the presence."

Sophie had to smile as she scrambled to her feet, and she climbed the steps without too much difficulty, Piers following behind. Their conversation still lingered in her mind and she was not as concerned about Brandt's reactions to her absence as she might have been.

But when they reached the top of the steps and walked up through the sloping garden to where Brandt awaited them, they found he was not alone. Another man was with him, a man of medium height and build, with dark brown hair, slightly winged with grey, and rather square attractive features. He was watching Sophie rather closely as she walked towards them and she wondered uneasily who he could be. What if this was someone who knew Eve, who recognized instantly that she was not Brandt St. Vincente's granddaughter?

But her fears in that direction were ungrounded. The identity of the stranger was soon revealed. Brandt took her arm quite possessively as she reached them, and said: "We've been waiting for you, Eve my dear. I invited Howard for tea to meet you, and then you didn't appear. Never mind. You're here now. I'd like to introduce you to a close friend of ours – Howard Fleming. Well, Howard? And what do you think of Jennifer's daughter?"

CHAPTER FOUR

SOPHIE dressed for dinner the following evening with some misgivings. They were going out for the evening, she and Brandt, Rosa and Edge, and she felt as nervous as a kitten. They were going to Comalee, to the Fleming house, and it loomed as forbiddingly as coming to Pointe St. Vincente had done.

The previous afternoon Howard Fleming had been charming. Far from treating her with the bitterness he must have felt towards Jennifer, he had behaved disarmingly, avoiding any of the pitfalls evident in their relationship. On the contrary, he had even gone so far as to express his sympathy at the death of her father, something which Brandt had not even done.

All the same, Sophie was conscious of her own position above all else, and while she might find Howard a friendly and attractive man, this was the man after all whom Jennifer had jilted in favour of James Hollister.

Now she turned from the mirror where she had been applying her make-up and crossed to the bed where she had laid the dress she was to wear that evening. It was the only formal evening dress she had brought with her and she hoped it was suitable for the occasion. It was a long-skirted cream gown of a lightweight material which looked like velvet and had been a parting gift from Eve. She had bought it for some special occasion but had not wanted to wear it again and so she had insisted that Sophie have it, and now she was glad she had accepted. The long-cuffed sleeves hid the faintly burned flesh of her forearms while the scooped neckline was both cooling and slightly sophisticated. With it she was wearing hooped silver earrings that swung and glinted in the smooth swathe of corn-gold hair. Altogether she was quite pleased with her appearance, and had she not been quaking in her shoes she might have looked forward to the occasion.

Piers was not accompanying them. He had, he said, other plans. He and Sophie had spent most of the day together, however, and she couldn't help but wish she could have counted on his uncomplicated presence this evening. But formal dinner dates were not his idea of fun and he planned to visit a discotheque in Port of Spain this evening in company with some of his friends.

Sophie descended the stairs just after seven and walked across the hall and into the lounge where the family usually gathered before dinner. But the room was deserted and she walked across to the windows rather thoughtfully, looking out on the shadowy garden beyond. A tray of drinks rested on a side table, but she had no desire to help herself even though Brandt had urged her to do so, and instead she walked to a long bookcase, partially filled with volumes, and began studying their titles. Like the rest of the house this was an extremely attractive room with soft brown leather chairs and an enormous couch upholstered in brown and white corded velvet. There were orange curtains at the windows and several small tables which Sophie suspected were quite irreplaceable, the bookshelves adding a comfortable, living-in appearance to the whole.

She had taken a volume from the shelves when she

heard footsteps behind her and turning found Edge St. Vincente just entering the room. In a white dinner jacket he looked quite magnificent, and Sophie felt a tremor of awareness slide unwillingly through her whole being. She thrust the book she had been holding back into its place and turned towards him reluctantly. But she could hardly remain standing with her back to him, could she?

His eyes moved over her appraisingly as they had done before and she quivered, and broke into nervous speech:

"Is – is it far to the Flemings' house?"

Edge moved further into the room, glancing towards the tray of bottles and glasses. "Not very," he replied coolly. "Do you want a drink?"

Sophie drew a trembling breath. "I don't mind."

"What, then?" He walked lazily towards the table.

Sophie hesitated. "Perhaps – sherry?"

He glanced over his shoulder at her. "Is that all you ever drink?" he enquired, rather derisively.

"Er – no. No. I – I sometimes have a gin and tonic."

He digested this without responding, but when he turned to hand her a glass she saw that it was not sherry but some amber-coloured liquid he was offering her. A tall glass, chinking with ice.

"What's this?" she asked, taking the glass with reluctance.

"Rum and Coke – a very small amount of rum," he added as she opened her mouth to protest. "You're a St. Vincente, remember. No St. Vincente worth her salt would settle for anything less."

"My surname – is Hollister," she declared unevenly, making no attempt to taste the drink he had given her.

"Is it?" His eyes mocked her over the rim of his own

glass which was as tall as hers but the liquid in it was colourless. "You're still sure about that?"

"What are you trying to say, Mr. – I mean – *Uncle* Edge?" It sounded unlikely, to say the least, the way she said it!

"Oh, nothing." He shook his head. "Drink your drink and enjoy it. You should relax more. Maybe then you wouldn't be so touchy when I tease you."

"Don't you mean *bait!*" retorted Sophie before she could stop herself, and a faint smile lifted the corners of his well-formed mouth.

But then there was the sound of voices from the hall and a moment later Brandt and Rosa entered the lounge. The older woman was wearing a long black chiffon gown that floated about her slightly angular figure and Sophie was glad she had taken trouble with her appearance. Obviously this was to be quite a formal occasion.

"Ah, you're ready," said Brandt, his eyes on Sophie with obvious admiration. "You look delightful, my dear. I shall be the envy of everyone there."

Sophie accepted the compliment shyly, looking awkwardly at the glass in her hand, and Brandt followed her gaze.

"I see you've been persuaded to try our local beverage," he remarked smilingly. "Good for you!"

There was nothing more Sophie could say. She was conscious of Edge's eyes upon her, but she refused to give him the satisfaction of witnessing her embarrassment, so she sipped some of the amber liquid and tried to look casual about it.

In fact, it was delicious, and after the first few tastes she found herself swallowing the rest without difficulty.

The spirit warmed the slightly cold feeling of nervousness that had invaded her stomach and gave her an added confidence as well. By the time they were ready to leave she felt much more prepared to face the evening ahead.

They drove to Comalee in a sleek grey limousine that Joseph, the black house servant, had brought to the foot of the steps for them. Edge chose to drive and Brandt sat beside him while Sophie and Rosa occupied the back. The sounds of the night creatures came through the opened windows of the car, strange and unfamiliar to Sophie's ears, while the scents of the flowers that grew in such profusion about the island had an intoxicating aroma all their own. There was no moon tonight, but the headlights of the car picked out pairs of eyes winking in the darkness, and spotlighted some exotic blossom growing wild at the roadside. Sophie felt curiously cool and detached and she decided that if that was what one rum punch woud do she had better not indulge herself too freely.

It took about twenty minutes to reach the gates of the Flemings' residence, and perhaps another three minutes to traverse the long curving drive. As they neared the house they could see the mass of lights ahead and hear the faint strains of calypso music.

There was another car parked on the curve of the drive and Edge brought the limousine to a smooth halt behind it and then slid out to help his aunt to alight. Brandt assisted Sophie and they all walked towards the lighted building together.

Shallow stone steps led up to a pillared portico where tubs of acacias tumbled in bright confusion. Beyond a paved terrace, lit by carriage lamps, grilled doors opened into a wide hall where the Flemings were greeting their guests with trays of canapés and glasses of champagne. As soon as Howard Fleming observed their arrival he came to greet them warmly, his gaze lingering openly on the attractive picture Sophie made.

"Come and meet my parents, Eve," he said, indicating that the others should accompany them. "My mother is longing to meet you."

Marion Fleming was as tall as her son with the same square-cut features and dark brown hair. Sophie thought she must be at least sixty, and yet she managed to look ten years younger. What was it about the air here that rejuvenated people's energies?

"So you're Jennifer's daughter," she exclaimed, by way of a greeting, examining Sophie with eyes that did not reflect the warmth of her words. "I'd never have guessed it. You're not at all like her."

"Nonsense!" That was Brandt, relieving Sophie of the necessity to reply to this awkward statement. "Of course she's like Jennifer. Perhaps you've forgotten how attractive Jennifer used to be."

"We haven't forgotten Jennifer, Brandt," retorted Marion, rather sharply, and for a moment there was an awkward silence.

But then Adrian Fleming, Howard's father, came forward to be introduced and in the small talk that followed the moment of unpleasantness was dissipated. Drinks were dispensed and Sophie found herself with a glass of champagne in one hand and a canapé in the other, with Howard Fleming at her side.

"You must forgive my mother, Eve," he murmured apologetically. "She's never really forgiven Jennifer for running away."

Sophie looked at him out of the corners of her eyes. "And have you, Mr. Fleming?"

"Call me Howard, please! Mr. Fleming sounds so formal, and surely we don't need to be formal with one another. Heavens, I might have been —" He broke off abruptly. "Tell me: what is it you do in England?"

Taking a deep breath, Sophie proceeded to tell him a little of what she knew of Eve's job, but fortunately his question had only been polite and very soon they moved on to less precarious subjects. Howard introduced her to their other guests, a middle-aged couple whose names were Laurence and Jean Kennedy, and to his sister, Janine.

Until that moment Sophie had scarcely been aware of Edge's presence, but when they moved across the room to find Howard's sister, they found her with Eve's uncle.

Janine Fleming possessed her brother's hair, thick and curly like an aureole about her head, but there the resemblance ended. She was smaller and slender with brilliant dark eyes and a petulant mouth. Dressed in a gown of glowing red chiffon, she was like a lick of flame against the whiteness of Edge's jacket, one slender arm draped possessively over his shoulder. When Howard brought Sophie to be introduced, she regarded her with scarcely concealed indifference; uttering a casual word of acknowledgement before continuing with what she had been saying to her companion. Edge's head was bent towards hers as he listened to what she had to say and Sophie felt an unreasoning twinge of anxiety stir within her at the apparent intimacy of their relationship. It was completely unexpected, and her nails curled into the palm of her hand as a sense of resentment swept over her. She didn't know why, but the idea that there might be something between

76

these two was quite distasteful to her. She suddenly found herself wondering what Edge's wife had been like and how long it was since she died.

She started to turn away, and as she did so she found Edge's eyes upon her. He was still presumably listening to what Janine was saying, but for a moment Sophie sensed his distraction. Turning her back on them, she tried to pay attention to what Howard was saying to her, but it was terribly difficult. Her hands were trembling, her palms were moist, and she despised the realization that Edge St. Vincente was responsible for this sudden rush of emotion. Heavens, what was she thinking of? Did she want to give him entirely the wrong impression? What would he think if he began to suspect that the girl who was supposed to be his niece was becoming aware of him in a way that was far from the innocent regard of a niece for her uncle?

She smoothed her hands over her thighs and gave Howard an unnecessarily grateful smile. But she must be mad to allow such thoughts free rein, she told herself fiercely. Indeed, she could never remember feeling this way before. She had never indulged in casual relationships, and had, perhaps foolishly, imagined herself free of the desires of the flesh. But just now she had had to acknowledge how small her experience must be, and how easy it could be to crave one man's attentions. She moved her shoulders impatiently. Well, she was aware of that weakness now and she would conquer it. But would she? probed a small voice. And why had she never felt this way towards any of the attractive men she had encountered in the course of her work, first at the television studios and then at the theatre? . . .

The Flemings' house was a much more conventional dwelling than the house at Pointe St. Vincente. In daylight, Howard told her, it was possible to see the sea from their upper windows, but they were some distance inland and consequently had had a pool installed in the gardens. Tonight the pool area was floodlit, and they dined outside at a long refectory table made attractive by bowls of scarlet and yellow hibiscus. The pool itself looked very inviting, and Howard suggested that Eve might like to come over and spend a day with them during her holiday. Sophie made some temporising comment to his invitation, but the idea was not wholly unappealing. Nevertheless, she wasn't at all sure what Marion Fleming's reactions to such an invitation might be, and although since that initial unpleasantness on their arrival she had behaved quite charmingly to all her guests there was something about the woman that Sophie didn't like.

Dinner was a delicious meal. Sophie had never tasted fish soup before, and the roast sucking pig gave the alfresco meal a barbecue flavour. They finished with fresh raspberries and some of the aromatically flavoured coffee which Sophie had really acquired a taste for. There was brandy, too, but this she refused. The rum punch Edge had given her before leaving had combined with the champagne to give her a sufficiently light-headed feeling, and she did not want to risk overdoing it. She was quite content to sit back in her seat between Brandt and Howard and listen to the conversation. The men were smoking the cigars which Adrian Fleming had provided and a haze of Havana tobacco smoke hung lazily in the air.

Across the table Edge was seated between Jean Kennedy and Janine Fleming. Sophie refused to allow her eyes to drift in that direction, although she couldn't help the speculative thought that Janine must have had some hand in the table placings.

When everyone was finished the table was quickly cleared and removed by the Flemings' house servants, and then more of the calypso music which they had heard earlier was provided by the record player. Janine dragged Edge up to dance with her and after Laurence Kennedy had escorted Marion Fleming on to the floor to join them, Howard turned to Sophie.

"I'm not very good at this modern stuff," he confessed, "but I'll do my best."

Sophie looked doubtfully at Brandt, seeking his approval, and he nodded his head encouragingly. "Go ahead, my dear," he urged. "I shall enjoy watching you."

For all Howard's protestations of ineptitude he proved to be quite an adequate dancer and Sophie enjoyed dancing with him. The music was slow and rhythmic, and he didn't hold her too tightly. She found herself pondering the curiousness of this situation had she really been Jennifer's daughter. After all, this man might have been her father if everything had gone according to plan, and she felt sure that that was what he had been about to say earlier when he had stopped himself. When the record ended, she was almost sorry, and was talking gaily to him as they walked back to the others.

Edge was standing by his father's chair now, talking with him and Adrian Fleming. Janine stood a little to one side, her petulant expression a little more pronounced, and Sophie guessed she was not used to being excluded from the conversation. But as it transpired that the men were discussing the accident which had holed the yacht Janine couldn't know much about it.

More drinks were served and Sophie accepted another glass of champagne with some misgivings. She was thirsty, though, after the exertion of dancing in a temperature that was still higher than she was used to, and it would have seemed churlish to refuse.

It seemed as though Howard had attached himself to her for the evening, and no matter where she went or who she spoke to he was never far from her side. Although she liked him and found him good company, she wished he would pay more attention to his mother's other guests. She was aware that Edge had noticed Howard's assiduity and she didn't care for the slightly derisive twist to his lips whenever he looked in their direction.

More records were put on the player and Laurence Kennedy invited Sophie to dance. She accepted after only a moment's hesitation and presently she saw that Edge was dancing with his hostess. Janine remained beside her brother and Brandt, but Sophie could tell from her expression that the situation was not to her liking.

Towards eleven-thirty after Sophie had had several more dances including one with Brandt and another with Adrian Fleming, there seemed a general move to break up the party. The Kennedys left insisting that they would be in touch with everyone to arrange another evening's entertainment at their home, and then Brandt and his sister accompanied the Flemings into the main building so that Rosa could collect her wrap. Sophie and Howard followed them, slightly ahead of Edge and Janine, and Sophie could hear the other girl whispering to him. Unfortunately, she couldn't hear what Janine was saying, and she had to force herself not to strain her ears to try and hear.

Good-byes were soon over and Sophie, Brandt and Rosa got into the sleek limousine for the homeward drive. Edge was slightly delayed, but after a moment he came striding over to take the driving seat and Sophie couldn't help but wonder whether Janine was responsible for the slightly grim expression he was wearing.

It was two days before Sophie saw Edge again.

The day after the party she learned he had left early that morning for Piarco, the international airport some miles outside of Port of Spain, to take a flight to Tobago. Piers told her that they had business interests in Scarborough, the island's small capital, and that now that his grandfather had virtually retired from the business, his father dealt with their interests himself.

"It sounds quite an exciting trip," murmured Sophie wistfully, scarcely aware that she had spoken aloud, and Piers looked at her in surprise.

"Would you have liked to have gone along, too?" he asked. "You could have done, I guess. I don't suppose my father thought it would interest you."

Sophie, who was seated beside him on a flat shelf of rock overlooking the pale green waters of the bay, her arms wrapped round her drawn-up knees, shook her head quickly. "Oh – oh, I was just musing," she exclaimed. "Besides, I'm quite happy here, thank you."

Piers grinned and stretched his brown body against the sun-warmed surface of the rock. "Yes, it is rather pleasant, isn't it? I don't dig this working bit. I'm much happier pottering about in the boats. Say!" He shot upright. "How'd you like to go sailing?"

81

"I don't – that is – I wouldn't know what to do," protested Sophie in alarm.

"I could teach you. It's easy really. So long as you can swim . . ."

"In case you capsize, you mean?" Sophie's eyes widened.

Piers gave her a wry smile. "Well, one has to be prepared for every eventuality."

Sophie examined one slender leg and thought how much more attractive it looked now that it was turning honey gold. "Oh, I don't know . . ." she murmured.

"Why? Don't you trust me?" Piers's eyebrows quirked and for a moment he looked disturbingly like his father.

Sophie looked away. "Of course I trust you. It's just – well, what will Brandt say?"

"Ask him."

"Shall I?" Sophie hesitated.

"I will, if you like."

"No. No, I'll do it." Sophie got to her feet and looked down at him, unselfconscious now of the briefness of her bikini. "Do I need shoes or sandals or anything?"

"Plimsolls, if you have them," replied Piers, standing up, too. "And hurry. You'll enjoy it."

Brandt offered no objections to their plans except to adjure Sophie to take care. "I don't want anything happening to you now that I've just found you," he said, rather emotionally, and Sophie felt terribly guilty. It was all right telling herself that had she not agreed to come he would have had no one on whom to lavish his affection and that therefore she was doing no harm, but she hated deceiving him like this. In that respect it got worse instead of better.

Piers took her out in the dinghy. Although it was a comparatively small craft it could move with alarming swiftness through the water, which Sophie found rather unnerving at first. But once she learned that sheets were ropes, and that the boom could give one a rather nasty blow if one did not duck out of its way, she began to enjoy herself. It was exciting and vastly more exhilarating than being power-driven, and as Piers explained what he was doing as they went along it was interesting, too.

"Dinghies sail fastest when they're kept in an almost upright position," he replied to Sophie's comment that she had seen yachts racing at very nearly right angles to their usual position. "The wind's the thing, of course, and that's why I keep the mainsheet loose in my hand so that I can ease it out to vary the width of sail into the wind. If there was a sudden strong gust that caught us unawares with too much sail showing we could capsize, so the helmsman always steers the craft as well as controlling the mainsail."

"Fascinating." Sophie looked up at the tall mast above them and the blue sky overhead. "Will I be able to steer the dinghy sometimes?"

Piers grimaced mockingly. "Not if you persist in leaning over the side like that. You're supposed to pull against the wind's pressure, not add your weight to it."

Sophie giggled and subsided into a safe position. "I'm glad you invited me to come."

"So am I." Piers looked at her with obvious pleasure. "We seem to get along together pretty well, don't we?"

Sophie nodded contentedly. It was true. When she was with Piers she could forget the invidiousness of her position and behave naturally. Maybe it was presumptuous on her behalf, but she felt that she and Piers would have hit it off anyway without the assumed ties of their relationship.

The following morning Brandt came into the morning room just as Sophie was finishing breakfast to tell her that Howard was on the phone wanting to speak with her. Sophie looked up and surprised a rather anxious expression on Brandt's face.

"Why?" she asked blankly, unable for the moment to think of any reason why Howard Fleming should want to speak to her.

Brandt shrugged his broad shoulders. "I think he wants to ask you to Comalee for the day," he replied heavily.

"Oh!" Sophie wiped her mouth slowly with her table napkin.

"Don't you want to go?" Brandt brightened.

She made an involuntary gesture. "Not particularly. I – I hardly know them."

"Then don't go." Brandt frowned. "Oh, I know Howard feels – well, drawn to you because you're Jennifer's daughter, but he can't expect you to take up where your mother left off!"

Sophie's eyes widened. "Do you think he feels that way?"

"Dammit, I know he does!" Brandt moved impatiently. "Surely even you noticed the way he hung about you the other evening!"

Sophie sighed. "I'd better tell him I can't go."

"Yes, I think perhaps you better had."

Sophie nodded and got to her feet. The last thing she

84

needed right now was for Howard Fleming to create emotional complications!

Howard was disappointed when she refused his invitation. "If you won't come for the whole day, let me take you out to dinner this evening," he suggested.

Sophie hesitated. "Er – Edge is away, as you probably know," she said at last. "I think – my grandfather would rather I was here this evening."

She heard Howard heave a deep sigh. "Tomorrow, then," he said insistently.

Sophie chewed uncomfortably at her lower lip. Short of telling him outright that she had no desire to make assignations with him or anyone else, what could she say?

"Edge comes back tomorrow, doesn't he?" Howard was saying now. "He and Brandt will have business matters to discuss tomorrow evening. Have dinner with me then."

Sophie considered this. There might be some truth in what he was saying. Piers had said it was a business trip, after all.

"All right," she agreed at last. "Tomorrow evening. What time?"

"I'll pick you up about seven, is that okay?"

"Fine." Sophie was already regretting the impulse which had made her agree to go out with him. "G'bye, then."

"Till tomorrow, Eve."

As she replaced the telephone receiver she became aware that she was no longer alone. Brandt had come out of the morning room and was standing watching her.

"You're going out with him tomorrow evening, then," he commented dourly, leaving her in no doubt that he had heard the end of her conversation with Howard.

She sighed. "What else could I do? Short of asking him to leave me alone?"

Brandt shook his head. "Where is he taking you?"

She shrugged. "I don't know. I didn't think to ask. Just out for a meal, I suppose."

"I see." Brandt thrust his hands into his trousers' pockets. "Well, I hope you know what you're doing." He moved nearer. "Do you realise, Eve, you've been here almost a week already and I don't feel we've ever really talked yet."

"Oh, we have!" Sophie made an eloquent gesture. "You know I'm – loving it here." That at least was the truth. "And everyone's been so – so kind."

"It's easy to be kind to someone like you, Eve," asserted Brandt huskily. "And you must realise that I – well –" he shook his head, "I simply don't want you to think of going back to England."

Sophie's lips parted. "But – but you know I must," she whispered uneasily.

"Why? Why must you?"

"I have – my work –"

"I know that. I'm prepared to accept what your career means to you. But if you want me to help you, surely it's not too much to expect that you spend some time here."

Sophie stared at him uncomprehendingly. "I don't understand," she began faintly, wondering with a sudden rush of intuition whether this was something else Eve had deliberately omitted to tell her.

"Of course you do." Fortunately Brandt was too intent on getting over his own point to pay much attention to her bewilderment. "Oh, I don't intend to discuss the pros and cons of the situation right now. There's plenty of time for that. But – well, I wish you'd think seriously of staying on here. Is a year too much to ask?"

"*A year?*"

This time Sophie's consternation was unmistakable, and Brandt hunched his shoulders disappointedly. "You don't want to," he said heavily. "And I can't force you. But I wish you'd try and see it my way."

"But I do see it your way!" Sophie pressed her palms together. "I – I understand perfectly. But – I have commitments, contracts! I can't just abandon everything for a *year*!"

Brandt exhaled noisily. "No, no, I can see that. I shouldn't have asked."

Sophie watched him helplessly, but what could she do? She was incapable of granting his wish even if she had wanted to do so. Eve's suggestion had been for two – maybe three weeks. Not a year! And besides, there was her own career to think of. The repertory company wouldn't keep her job open for ever.

All the same, had she really been Eve Hollister, had Brandt really been her grandfather, she knew that nothing would have stopped her from remaining here, from doing exactly as he wanted. Already her life in England had become vague and colourless, while Trinidad, and Pointe St. Vincente in particular, were the realities . . .

CHAPTER FIVE

EDGE arrived back late the following afternoon and was immediately closeted with Brandt in his study. Sophie didn't expect to see him before leaving with Howard, but when she came downstairs at about a quarter to seven she found him in the lounge, helping himself to a drink. He was still wearing the casual clothes he had worn to travel in, and his expression was grim when he turned and found her hovering in the doorway.

Sophie advanced cautiously into the room, absurdly conscious of the limitations of her simple linen dress, and attempted a casual: "Have a good trip?"

Edge swallowed half the contents of his glass before replying. "Successful," he conceded dryly.

"Oh – good." Sophie linked her fingers. "I expect you're tired."

"No. Should I be?" He was deliberately obtuse.

Sophie turned away. When he chose to be like this she had no defence against him.

"I understand you're having dinner with Howard." His words caused her to half turn towards him again.

"Yes. He should be here soon."

"If you want my advice, you'll stay clear of Howard," Edge remarked distinctly.

Sophie felt nervousness dissolving beneath a surge of pure anger. "I don't recall asking for your advice."

"No, but I'm offering it anyway."

"Why? Why shouldn't I go out with him?" Sophie

clenched her fists, determinedly putting aside her own earlier doubts about the advisability of getting involved with Howard.

"He's too old for you for one thing," retorted Edge, replacing his glass on the tray. "And for another he's suffering from the delusion of imagining that you're the reincarnation of Jennifer."

Sophie drew a trembling breath. "We – we're friends, that's all."

"Really?" Edge reached for a cigar from the box on the mantelshelf and put it between his teeth. "Well, don't say I didn't warn you!"

Sophie sighed, watching him as he lit the cigar and inhaled deeply. "I wish you'd stop talking like this," she exclaimed. "You're my – my uncle, after all."

He hooked his thumbs into the low belt of his pants. "So how would you like me to be?"

Sophie bent her head. "Just don't – don't bait me all the time."

"Oh, I see. You can't stand the pace, is that it?"

She looked up. His eyes were hard and there was a mocking twist to his mouth. "Thank goodness Piers isn't like you," she burst out impulsively.

"Isn't he? Isn't he just? Are you sure of that?"

"Of course I'm sure. I enjoy being with him."

"And you don't enjoy being with me?"

"Stop putting words into my mouth!"

"I thought the implication was unavoidable."

"You think you're so clever, don't you?"

"Not particularly. It was a reasonable observation."

"Oh!" She turned away with a frustrated gesture. She simply couldn't win an argument against such implacable opposition. "I think you like – hurting me."

Edge rested his arm along the mantelshelf. "I wouldn't say that –"

"Well, I would!" Sophie's mouth worked tremulously. "Why can't you speak to me without being so damnably sarcastic all the time?"

"Is that what I am?"

"You know it is!"

Edge shrugged his broad shoulders lazily, the movement drawing Sophie's attention to the hard muscles beneath the thin cotton shirt he was wearing. "If I stop being – to use your own words – so damnably sarcastic to you, will you stay away from Howard?"

Sophie's dark brows lifted in surprise. "You mean – you mean refuse to go out with him?"

"Not tonight. The arrangement's made, and it stands. I mean – don't accept any future invitations."

Sophie made a confused gesture. "But why?"

Edge's eyes narrowed. "It's a straightforward request, answer it!"

"But what could I say? It would sound so – so rude –"

"Tell him you've made other arrangements. Tell him you're going out with me."

"With you?" Sophie was astounded. "But he'd know it wasn't true."

"I should make sure it was."

"But why should you do this –"

"Howard's my friend. I don't want to see him hurt a second time. Not if I can help it."

Sophie hesitated. "What makes you so sure I would hurt him?"

"You're going back to England, aren't you? When this

90

charade is over?"

"What do you mean — *charade?*" Her heart pounded wildly.

"It was a term, that was all. And after all, it is a charade really, isn't it? I mean — the whole situation?"

Sophie didn't know how to reply, but luckily at that moment they both heard the sound of a car's engine as the vehicle descended the slope to the courtyard outside.

"This sounds like the man himself," remarked Edge dryly. "Don't distress yourself. One of the servants will let him in."

Sophie shook her head. "I wish I wasn't going anywhere," she declared unevenly.

Edge shrugged and straightened. "Why? You'll probably enjoy yourself."

"After this?" Sophie was aghast.

"Yes. Put this conversation to the back of your mind."

"As if I could!"

"All right, remember it, then." Edge sounded impatient. "Just don't make any plans for tomorrow, will you? Because I'm taking you to Genevra."

"Genevra?" Sophie's eyes widened. "Where's that?"

"It's a small cove, some distance along the coast. It's only accessible by sea and the bay is calm and quite shallow. I thought you might like to try your hand at snorkelling."

"Snorkelling?" Sophie felt a faint stirring of excitement. "It sounds — interesting."

"It is." The voice was Piers'. Turning to the door, Sophie saw he had just entered the room behind her. "Has Dad been telling you about tomorrow's proposed outing?"

Sophie's lips parted. "You – know?"

"Of course."

"Oh, I see." Suddenly the prospective trip lost a little of its appeal. "Are you coming, too?"

"Try to stop me!" Piers was exuberant. "I can't wait to show you what it's like under the surface."

Sophie nodded, managing a slight smile, conscious of Edge's eyes upon her. Their conversation had really had nothing to do with his decision to take her out. No doubt his father had suggested it. He, too, wanted to keep her away from Howard.

One of the maids came to the lounge door. "Mr. Fleming is here, Mr. Edge," she announced. "He's come for Miss Eve."

"Ask him to come in, Rachel," ordered Edge calmly, stubbing out the butt of his cigar in a heavy onyx ashtray. "Will you have a drink before you leave, Eve?"

Sophie had little chance to make any response before Howard Fleming entered the room. In a dark brown lounge suit, he looked suave and stockily attractive, his well-dressed appearance contrasting sharply with Edge's casual, travel-stained attire. And yet for all that, if she was really honest with herself, Sophie had to admit that she would rather have remained home this evening and avoided the inevitable *tête-à-tête* with the man who had once expected to marry Jennifer . . .

But although she had not expected to do so, Sophie did enjoy her evening out. Howard took her to a nightclub in Port of Spain, and after a delicious meal they watched limbo dancers and listened to more of the stirring steel music played by the bands rehearsing for the coming carnival. There was such an air of uninhibited excitement about the whole proceedings that no one could have remained unmoved by it, and Sophie found herself keeping time with the music and longing to dance. She envied the women who joined the band on the floor, swinging and swaying to the rhythm with sensuous abandon, and wondered what Howard would think if she were to cast her inhibitions aside and follow their example. She sensed he would not approve. Although he seemed a likeable, rather amiable man, she was aware of a certain restraint about him which would curtail any urge he had to act impulsively. Her awareness of this aspect of his character was an instinctive thing, and she couldn't help speculating whether this restraint had been in any way responsible for Jennifer's behaviour years ago.

Afterwards they drove home through the velvety softness of the night air, and Howard pointed out the twinkling lights of Venezuela just visible in the distance. They had talked quite a lot throughout the evening, casual conversations about music and films, and books they both enjoyed, but the journey home was accomplished almost in silence and Sophie wondered what occupied Howard's thoughts. Her own were busy with the prospect of the day ahead, and she couldn't deny the surge of excitement that its knowledge brought her. She refused to speculate on the possible innuendo behind Edge's barbed comments, and contented herself with the assurance that had he suspected she was not who she said she was he would have exposed her by now.

When Howard brought the car to a halt in the courtyard of the St. Vincente house he switched off the engine and turning to her, said: "I've enjoyed this evening so much, Eve. Please say you'll come over to Comalee to-morrow."

Sophie slid into her corner, as far away from him as was possible in the confines of the car, and shook her head apologetically. "I'm afraid I can't," she said, and was glad that she did not have to lie about it. "My – my uncle and Piers are taking me sailing."

"Edge?" Howard's brows drew together in surprise. "I understood he and Janine were spending the day together."

"Janine?" murmured Sophie faintly.

"Sure. My sister. You've surely realised how things are between those two?"

Sophie caught her breath, disguising the small sound in a cough. "No. How are they?" she asked softly.

Howard sighed, running his fingers round the rim of the steering wheel. "Well, I guess they'll get married one day. There's no hurry. They've known one another long enough not to be in any rush."

"I – didn't know that." Sophie hoped she didn't sound as shocked as she felt.

Howard shrugged. "It's such common know-ledge around here, I don't suppose anyone saw any necessity to tell you. But since Gerry died –"

"Gerry?"

"Geraldine St. Vincente, Edge's wife. Your late aunt, I suppose."

"Oh, I see. I – I'm afraid my knowledge of the family is rather limited."

"It would be," Howard nodded. "And of course, no one talks much about her these days. It's almost ten years since she died."

Sophie opened her mouth to ask more questions about the unknown Geraldine, and then closed it again. It was no business of hers. Even less when you considered that she had no real place in this family. "You said – since Gerry died ..." she prompted him, unable to leave it alone entirely.

"What?" Howard frowned. "Oh, yes, well – since Gerry died, Janine has been his shadow. She's only about your age, of course, little more than a kid when Edge became a widower, but she always adored him, and – well, I guess Edge understands her."

"I see." Sophie felt slightly nauseated. Those oysters they had had this evening couldn't have agreed with her. "Well, I must be going."

Howard sighed. "And you won't change your mind about tomorrow?"

"I can't." Sophie shook her head.

Howard nodded. "Okay. I'll ring you. In a few days, hm? Maybe we can arrange a date that's suitable to both of us."

Taking the cowardly way out, Sophie allowed it to go at that, searching urgently for the door catch. It suddenly swung open and she scrambled out, only to find that Howard had walked round and opened the door for her.

"Goodnight, then," she said, with an awkward proffering of her hand, but Howard merely smiled and bending touched her forehead with his lips.

"Goodnight, Eve," he said, and walked back to get into his car, leaving her feeling more guilty than before.

Brandt came to meet her as she let herself into the hall of the house. "Well?" he said. "Have you had a good evening?"

"Very good, thank you." Sophie's voice was low and Brandt looked at her sharply.

"What's wrong? You look pale." His eyes darkened. "Howard didn't –"

"Howard didn't do anything," declared Sophie quickly. "I – I just feel a bit sick, that's all. Too much rich food, I suppose."

"Hmm." Brandt sounded sceptical. "Well, come into the lounge and have a drink before you go to bed."

Sophie was about to refuse, but then the thought of her quiet bedroom changed her mind. Right now, she didn't want to examine her thoughts too closely. She preceded Brandt into the attractive lamplit room and found to her relief that it was empty.

"What will you have?" Brandt went to the tray of drinks. "Brandy, gin, rum?"

"Nothing like that, really." Sophie sank down into the soft contours of the couch. "Just some orange juice, please."

"Is that the sort of thing you want if you feel sick?"

"Well, I'm sure it's no more lethal than the others," exclaimed Sophie, managing a faint smile. "Er – where is everyone?"

"Rosa and Piers are in bed. Edge hasn't come in yet."

"He's out?" Sophie hoped she didn't sound too curious.

"Yes. He's over at the Flemings."

Sophie swallowed hard and accepted the glass Brandt handed her, looking down into it concentratedly. "Howard – told me that – that Edge and Janine . . ."

Brandt clicked his tongue impatiently. "Oh, yes? Well, I shouldn't pay too much attention to what Howard says."

"Why not?" Sophie looked up in surprise.

"The Flemings have been trying to link themselves with this family for years, since long before your mother's time. I don't expect Edge to marry Janine."

"But why? Doesn't he love her, is that what you're saying?"

"Love doesn't come into it." Brandt shook his head. "Dear Eve, what an innocent you are in some ways! Quite different from my impressions of female journalists." Sophie flushed, but fortunately he didn't appear to notice as he went on: "If I've learned one thing about my children, my dear, it's that they don't like to be coerced into doing anything. If Edge ever does decide to marry again, and quite honestly I can't see any likelihood of that, he'll do the running for himself. Janine is far too persistent in that direction. She went to Tobago with him, you know."

Sophie's fingers tightened round her glass. "But – you just said –"

"Well, perhaps I phrased that rather badly. She went to Tobago on the same plane as he did, and stayed at the same hotel."

"You mean – without an invitation?"

Brandt smiled. "Janine is a very determined young woman."

"I know, but – but –"

"– but you'd never do a thing like that?" he finished.

"Well, yes."

"Perhaps it's just that the right man hasn't yet come along to turn your world upside-down," he commented dryly. "I'm pretty sure your mother would have done something drastic if I'd stopped her from going off with your father."

97

It was the first time since her arrival that he had spoken of the elopement and Sophie wondered whether her presence here was helping him to view that situation with less bitterness. If it were so, then at least she had achieved something.

But Brandt's next words disabused that belief.

"You don't really remind me of either of your parents," he remarked. "Your father was never one to miss an opportunity."

Sophie bent her head. "He – he loved my mother, you know," she ventured.

Brandt sighed. "Did he? But he didn't make her happy. Perhaps if she hadn't died when you were born, things would have been different ..." His voice trailed away. "But it's too late now. We must try and forget the past and make the best use we can of the present."

Sophie let it go at this. It was obvious that talking about his daughter could still upset him. She wondered for the first time what he would have made of Eve. In her determination to get what she wanted whom did she resemble? Jennifer, who ran away for love – or James, who defied this arrogant old man to marry the woman of his choice?

Swallowing the remainder of her orange juice she got to her feet. "Time for bed, I think."

Brandt nodded, his expression gentle. "Try not to think too badly of me," he murmured, as she went past him.

Sophie halted, arrested by the agony in his voice. "Oh, please," she said, putting a hand on his arm. "Like you said, it's all in the past. It doesn't do to bear grudges."

"Thank you, my dear." Brandt sounded emotional. "You get along to bed now. You're going out with Edge and Piers tomorrow, aren't you?"

"That's right." Sophie squeezed his arm gently. "Goodnight, Brandt," she whispered, and on impulse she leant forward and pressed her lips against his cheek. But even before she drew back again she sensed they were no longer alone. She hadn't heard a car, but that was not so surprising when one could allow a vehicle to cruise down the slope to the house. And now Edge stood in the doorway regarding them intently, the twist of cynicism marring his disturbingly attractive features.

CHAPTER SIX

THE shallow waters of Genevra Cove lapped gently on sands bleached white by the heat of the sun. It was every bit as secluded and inaccessible as Edge had described, with tall, moss-covered cliffs towering above like the bastions of some mediaeval fortress. The dinghy had been beached some distance from where Sophie was lying, and for the moment she was alone. Completely alone, she thought wryly, wondering what she would do if for some unforeseen reason Edge and Piers did not come back. She could not sail the dinghy, and it had no engine. And there was no earthly chance of her being able to climb the cliffs. She would be marooned!

Rolling on to her stomach, she pillowed her head on her folded arms. Of course they would come back. Edge was going to teach her how to use the snorkel. At present he and Piers had gone into deeper water with the use of the scuba diving gear, but Edge had said that she would need more experience of swimming under water before she tackled that. Sophie doubted she ever would. After all, she had been here over a week already, and sooner or later she would have to start thinking about making arrangements for her flight back to England. She was putting off mentioning such a thing to Brandt for obvious reasons, but if she was wholly honest with herself she would admit that the idea of leaving Pointe St. Vincente enveloped her in depression. She didn't want to leave. Apart from the beauty of her surroundings, she had become fond of Brandt and Piers. Her feelings about Edge did not bear thinking about.

With an impatient exclamation she levered herself up on to her knees and sat for a moment in that position watching the antics of a sand crab making its awkward way up the beach. She was beginning to see that this masquerade which Eve had persuaded her to play could have repercussions which might conceivably destroy any chance of happiness she might have had.

Trying to thrust these disturbing thoughts aside, she rose abruptly to her feet, curving her arms to lift the weight of her hair from her neck. The warmth of the sun was like a balm to her troubled spirits and she stretched with lissom grace, unaware until it was too late that she was being observed. Edge had come up out of the water at the far end of the beach and was presently shedding his oxygen tanks into the bottom of the dinghy.

Immediately and defensively Sophie's arms dropped to her sides and she bent to shake the sand out of her towel. Anything to avoid the crazy impulse she had that made her want to meet his eyes, to look at him and admire that lean, tanned body in the brief navy swimming shorts. He came across the sand towards her, treading with difficulty in rubber flippers so that Sophie was able to hide her embarrassment in laughter.

"You're not the Penguin, by any chance, are you?" she teased him, and he looked down at his feet good-naturedly.

"I've got some for you, too. And here's the mask and the snorkel. Do you think you can manage to put them on?"

Sophie subsided on to the sand again. "I'll try. Where's Piers?"

"He'll be back shortly. He knows I've left him."

Sophie nodded and began pulling on the rubber flippers. They went on quite easily, but when she tried to stand up again it was harder than she thought. It was difficult to avoid standing on the rubber fin of the other foot, and after watching her struggle for a minute, Edge bent and offered her his hand. Sophie took it willingly and he pulled her up sharply, releasing her almost immediately.

"Now!" Edge handed her the face mask. "Put this on — no, over the bridge of your nose, like this." He adjusted it for her. "This is the snorkel. You see, this piece goes into your mouth and the tube is secured on the side of the face mask — there."

Sophie nodded, trying the wide piece of rubber in her mouth. She pulled it out again and grimaced. "It's awfully big, isn't it?"

"Not really. You're nervous, that's all." Edge was patient. More patient than Sophie would have expected. "Now, try again. You see this little ball in the end of the snorkel? Well, so long as you're breathing naturally it stays here. But if you start panicking it cuts off your air supply and you have to surface, right?"

"How will I know?" Sophie was aghast.

"Oh, you'll know," Edge assured her dryly. "Shall we try it?"

The water, particularly near the beach, was very warm, but Sophie found herself shivering with apprehension.

"Relax!" advised Edge, wading out and plunging his whole body underwater. "There's nothing to be afraid of."

"I – I know." Sophie examined the mouthpiece of the snorkel before venturing to put it between her lips. "But what are you going to do? I thought you were coming with me, but you don't have any equipment."

"I am coming with you, and I don't need any equipment," Edge assured her, pushing his wet hair back with a careless hand. "Now – start swimming, and when I tell you try to swim just below the surface of the water. Keep your face down and breathe naturally."

Sophie did as she was told. It wasn't too bad at first. She was concentrating on following Edge's instructions implicitly, and besides, the gorgeous colours of sea anemones and other marine plant life fascinated her. Tiny tropical fish swam within touching distance and darted about amongst coral rocks that reflected the rainbow colours of the sun on water. She was conscious of Edge swimming beside her and she felt safe.

But then he swam some distance ahead and when Sophie realized that she was out of her depth she moved her feet more rapidly to catch up with him. Unfortunately, the flippers drove her downward into the water and the air-tube was blocked and her mouth filled with salt water. Momentarily she panicked and came up threshing wildly, coughing and choking and gasping for breath.

Immediately, it seemed, Edge was beside her, speaking reassuringly to her, one arm securing her against him while he removed the offending mask and snorkel from her face. Sophie was trembling violently, but as her panic subsided and common sense returned she became aware of the hard strength of his muscles against her.

"Do you want to go back?" he asked against her ear as her breathing became normal again, but Sophie shook her head.

"I'm – all right now," she murmured unsteadily, and without another word he released her.

She turned to face him. "Can – can you help me put the mask on again?" she asked, as he offered the things to her. "I – I'm not absolutely sure how it goes on."

Edge gave an assenting movement of his head and came closer. "Put your hands on my shoulders," he said briefly. "I can't get any leverage if you keep moving away."

Sophie put her hands on his shoulders and he quickly slipped the mask into place, offering her the mouthpiece to insert. "Thank you," Sophie managed a smile. "I'm sorry I was so stupid."

"You weren't stupid," retorted Edge, rather cuttingly. "Just inexperienced, that's all."

Sophie made an upward movement of her shoulders and put the mouthpiece to her lips. Then she took a deep breath and started swimming again. This time Edge stayed beside her, but after about fifteen minutes he indicated that they should go back. Sophie wanted to protest, but she didn't dare, and she swam obediently after him, standing up when he did to wade out of the water.

Piers was back now and Sophie unpacked the lunch which Violet had provided for them. There was cold chicken and ham, salads and sweet potatoes, fresh fruit and wine. There were also several cans of beer which earlier Piers had secured inside a string bag and placed in the water near where the dinghy was beached for coolness.

Afterwards, it was pleasant just relaxing in the shade of an overhanging rock and allow the blistering heat of the day to burn itself out. Piers rested for only a short time before padding along the beach to mess about in the dinghy, and Sophie was left with only Edge for company. She had thought he was asleep, but when she got up on her haunches to smooth her towel his eyes opened and he pushed the dark glasses he was wearing up his forehead.

"Did I disturb you?" Sophie was apologetic. "I didn't mean to."

Edge shook his head lazily. "I wasn't asleep."

"Oh! Oh, good." Sophie subsided on to her towel again, drawing her legs up and resting her elbows on her knees.

Unexpectedly his hand brushed her bare hip and she jumped violently, turning to look at him in surprise. "Don't be so jumpy," he commented dryly. "I was only knocking a fly away. What did you think I was about to do?"

Sophie had turned bright red. Her reactions had been totally out of proportion to the minuteness of the incident and she felt terribly embarrassed. "I – I didn't know what it was, that was all," she defended herself uncomfortably. "You startled me."

"Did I? I'm sorry." But the mocking note was back in his voice again and Sophie turned back to her contemplation of the ocean, her shoulders hunched resentfully. "I'd forgotten how touchy you are where I'm concerned."

Sophie clenched her fists. "Oh, don't flatter yourself!" she exclaimed furiously, not looking at him. "I'm not about to swoon just because Edge St. Vincente has laid a hand on me!"

Edge stretched his length more comfortably against the warm sand. "I don't know what you mean," he commented mildly.

"Yes, you do." She cupped her chin on her balled fists. "The apparent effect you have on some women can't have passed entirely unnoticed, I'm sure."

"By whom?"

"By you, of course." Sophie glanced round at him coldly.

"I see." Edge took the dark glasses off altogether and examined them. "As – er – as my niece, you feel I have an inflated opinion of myself, is that it?"

Sophie hesitated, aware that she was getting into deep water. "Oh – does it matter?" she muttered, half to herself.

"I think so, yes." Edge laid the dark glasses aside and studied her averted head. "I want to hear more about this opinion you've formed of me. Are you sure you're being – objective?"

Sophie dug her fingers into the sand. "I don't see that there's any point in discussing it further."

"Don't you?" Edge ran his hand exploringly across the hair-roughened expanse of his chest. "But I want to. You intrigue me. How can someone in your position appreciate whether or not I am attractive to women?"

Sophie wished she had held her tongue and never started this conversation. "It – it's obvious," she began uncomfortably.

"Is it?" Edge jack-knifed into a sitting position and looked sideways at her. "Tell me!"

Sophie moved her shoulders helplessly. "You're doing it again, aren't you?" she accused him frustratedly. "Baiting me, I mean." She looked along the beach to where Piers was seated in the dinghy doing something

106

to the sails. "It's just as well your son can't hear you."

"Why?" Edge tipped his head to one side provocatively. "What have I said that he shouldn't hear?"

Sophie shook her head, unable to think of any reply. She looked along at him. This close she could see the yellow flecks in his amber eyes, the thick length of his lashes, the firmness of his jaw muscle. His hair was very dark in the sun, his sideburns accentuating his tan. Her lips parted involuntarily as his expression became more intent and eventually she had to look away, half shocked at the feelings he aroused in her. When one of his fingers trailed deliberately down the curve of her thigh and calf, her nerves tightened unbearably and she could hardly breathe. She ought to stop him, she knew that, but there was something sensual and stimulating about that forbidden caress, and she acknowledged with a sense of dismay that she wanted him to go on touching her.

"You're becoming quite brown," he murmured, withdrawing his fingers. "It suits you."

Sophie gulped as sanity reasserted itself. "Wh – what are you trying to do, *Uncle* Edge? Demonstrate your expertise with women on me?"

Edge's eyes darkened angrily, and his hand shot across, savagely imprisoning her forearm. "Have a care – *Eve!*" he bit out grimly. "Perhaps my scruples bother me less than yours!"

"What do you mean?"

"I mean that you might conceivably get more than you bargained for when you came here!"

"You – you can't frighten me –"

"Can't I?" His thumb moved insistently against her flesh. "I think I could. In fact I'm sure of it."

"Let go of my arm! You're annoying me."

"Am I?" Edge's eyes glittered dangerously. "Don't you dare to try and tell me what to do!"

"Why not? Does it ruin the image?"

Sophie didn't know what was driving her on to speak to him this way, taunting him. She knew she was dicing with danger, but she was unaccountably excited by the knowledge that she could get under his skin, if only slightly.

Struggling on to her knees, she tried to prise his fingers from her arm, but they were immovable and in desperation she dug her nails into his wrist. The unexpected pain she inflicted caused Edge to utter an oath and release her so abruptly that she lost her balance and fell back on the sand. Edge recovered instantly from the scratch she had inflicted on his wrist, and before she had the chance to put any distance between them he had flung himself on her, pressing her arms back behind her head.

"You little she-cat!" he muttered furiously, his face contorted with rage. "You deserve everything you get!"

Sophie was really frightened now. She struggled with him, but it was futile. He had control now and he knew it. He was astride her, his knees digging into the outer rim of her rib-cage, a perfect example of male dominance. She was breathing quickly, shallow choking breaths that caused her breasts to rise and fall tremblingly beneath the thin bra of her bikini. She turned her head desperately to see whether Piers had observed their confrontation, but he was seated calmly in the dinghy, his back towards them. She would have to shout to attract his attention, and what would be his reaction if he saw them?

She heaved a heavy sigh and then, without warning, she

was free. Edge got to his feet to stand over her for a minute, and then he turned away, the anger in his face giving way to contempt, but whether for himself or her she could be sure.

Sophie lay on the sand, still stunned by the events of the last few minutes, but Edge had evidently had enough of her company, because he strode away across the sand towards the dinghy, leaving her feeling more alone than she had ever felt in her life before.

Sophie had plenty of time during the next two days to ponder the events of that disastrous day out. Much against his father's wishes, Edge had decided on the spur of the moment to pilot the charter vessel due to sail the following morning on a two day's fishing trip, and Piers had been only too eager to accompany him. The yacht had been hired over a week ago by a Venezuelan business man and his wife, but Sophie was aware that Edge had only chosen to go to avoid her. She told herself she was glad, that to be free of his sarcastic presence would be a pleasure, but she knew she was deceiving herself. In spite of everything that had happened between them, she was becoming more and more involved with him, mentally at least, and there had been times on that homeward journey from Genevra Cove when she had been tempted to go to him and apologise for her behaviour and beg his forgiveness. But of course, she had not done so, and now he had left her again.

Without even Piers' companionship, Sophie spent less time swimming, wandering about the elegantly furnished rooms of the house aimlessly. She knew she ought to broach the subject of her leaving with Brandt, but the idea of putting such things into words seemed so final somehow.

All the same, it had to be done. The sooner she was away from here, away from Edge's disruptive presence, the better. The amount of freedom she had here had made her imaginative. Once she was back in Sandchurch, organizing things at the repertory playhouse, she would forget all about this stupid compulsion she felt towards a man who imagined she was his niece.

On the morning after Edge and Piers' departure, she and Brandt had breakfast together which was an unusual occurrence but which Brandt had contrived because the others were away. Sophie thought the situation presented an ideal opportunity, and with some misgivings she mentioned that it was time she made some enquiries about the availability of flights back to England.

She was not prepared for Brandt's reactions, however. He thrust back his chair to stand before her militantly, his hands clenched at his sides.

"You can't be serious!" he declared roughly.

Sophie blinked. "Why not?"

"Why not? *Why not?*" Brandt had a muscle working in his jaw. "Because I won't allow it, that's why not."

Sophie tried to remain calm. "Brandt, I've got to go."

He bent forward to rest the palms of his hands on the table in front of him, staring at her with piercing blue eyes. "Only a few days ago I asked you whether you'd consider staying here a year, Eve," he said grimly. "Now you come to me, after being here less than a fortnight, and calmly say you're going to make enquiries about leaving! How do you expect me to take that?"

Sophie felt an overwhelming sense of compassion. If

only she could tell him how much she wanted to stay. "But – but, Brandt, I only planned to stay two or three weeks –" she protested, forcing herself to say the words that Eve expected her to say.

"But that was before we met – before we got to know one another. I thought – I imagined, foolishly perhaps, that you were beginning to like it here – to like *me*!"

Sophie gazed up at him helplessly. "Oh, Brandt, I do like you," she exclaimed with feeling. "You know I do. You've been so kind to me, and I shall miss you – terribly."

"Then don't go!" Brandt straightened from the table. "It's as simple as that."

"No, it's not." Sophie wondered how she could make him understand without hurting him. "I couldn't give up my work for a year and then expect to take it up again without a great deal of difficulty –"

"Yes, well, that's what we have to talk about, isn't it?"

Sophie's brows drew together. "I don't understand."

"Now, Eve, don't let's pretend about this. You knew when you came here that I'd do anything I could to keep you here, and even if it means providing the means to open your own agency, then I'm prepared to do it."

Sophie was aghast. Suddenly she was remembering something else Brandt had said once before, something about him being prepared to help her, which of course meant help Eve. But in that way? At the time it had seemed relatively unimportant, but now Sophie found herself wondering exactly on what terms had Eve said she would come to Trinidad? And why had she mentioned none of this to her, Sophie?

Of course, the answer to that was plain. Had Sophie suspected there was anything more to this than the kind of mercy dash Eve had played it out to be, she would have turned it down flat, and Eve had known that. But was it possible that Eve's desire that she should not disappoint her grandfather had some more material motive? The idea was cheap and unpalatable, and Sophie wondered exactly what kind of a situation she had got herself into. The only thing she could do was to cable Eve and ask her to write and tell her exactly what she hoped to gain from this deception.

She suddenly realized that Brandt was still waiting for her to reply, and shaking her head a trifle bemusedly, she said: "I don't expect you to have to do anything like that. I – I'm not holding out for mercenary reasons, believe me. It's just that – well, I have to go back."

"But not after two weeks!" protested Brandt heavily.

Sophie tucked the swathe of heavy hair behind her ears. "Well –" she began slowly. "Perhaps I could stay – three weeks –"

"Four!" said Brandt determinedly.

"I'm not bargaining with you," Sophie cried, shaking her head.

"But you will stay a month," stated Brandt, with decision. "Won't you?"

For the rest of the day, Sophie regretted the impulse which had made her agree. After all, the leave of absence she had obtained had only been for three weeks at the most, and there was still the problem of Eve to consider. Somehow she would have to get into Port of Spain and send that cable without anyone's observation. Eve could always write to her here without fear of discovery, but Sophie could hardly be observed addressing a cable, apparently to herself, to Eve's flat in London without arousing a great deal of speculation.

Edge and Piers arrived back that evening while Sophie, Brandt and Rosa were having dinner on the terrace. They came to the opened french doors leading on to this balcony which overlooked the shoreline to announce their return, and Sophie couldn't deny the surge of reassurance she felt at knowing they were safely home again. In salt-water-stained jeans, a creased denim battle jacket opened to the waist, a two days' growth of beard on his chin, Edge still managed to look lazily attractive, and she wondered whether the Venezuelan's wife had thought so, too.

"Everything go smoothly?" enquired Brandt, getting up to greet them.

"Great!" Piers nodded vigorously. "We caught a barracuda! Man, that was some fish!"

Edge listened to his son enthusing with a look of laconic tolerance on his face. It wasn't the first time Sophie had noticed the casual affection that existed between them, and it caused a twinge of envy in the pit of her stomach.

"I was a reasonably successful trip," Edge was agreeing calmly. "Plenty of smaller fish and a couple of tarpon. Apart from Maria falling overboard, it was a pretty good charter."

Brandt's hand gripped his shoulder. "Who fell overboard?"

"Diego's wife – Maria. She was so excited about the barracuda, she nearly provided a meal for it instead of the other way about."

Sophie listened to this jealously. She might have known that there would always be a woman on Edge's horizon.

"And is she all right?" Brandt was obviously con-

113

cerned. "She didn't get injured?"

Piers shook his head. "Heck, no! Dad dived in and hauled her out. It was her own fault. Her old man was absolutely furious with her, wasn't he, Dad?"

Edge moved his shoulders indifferently. "No sweat. She was all right. Wet and shaken, that's all." His gaze seemed to move deliberately towards Sophie. "Women tend to panic, unfortunately."

Sophie looked down at the unfinished lobster on her plate. Her appetite had depleted rapidly and she inwardly chided herself for caring about anything Edge did or said. Why couldn't she regard him like she regarded Brandt — or Piers? She was fond of both of them and they both seemed quite fond of her, so why was Edge different? The truth was, she acknowledged, she had been aware of him in a way hitherto unknown to her since their first meeting in the hotel bar in Port of Spain.

Brandt wanted to hear more about the trip, but Edge excused himself, saying he must have a shower and a change of clothes and Brandt returned to the table. He shook his head as he re-tackled the shellfish on his plate.

"Imagine that!" he exclaimed, addressing himself to no one in particular. "Falling overboard indeed! I always said women aboard charter vessels were bad news!"

Sophie pretended to show an interest in her own food, but she longed to know more about the Venezuelan woman. "Do — do you know these people?" she ventured, as casually as she could.

Brandt frowned. "The Diegos? Well, not personally. I know them, of course. Rafael Diego is in the oil business, just as we are. Edge has had dealings with him before. Why?"

"I just wondered." Sophie bent her head. "Are they – I mean – they are friends of his?"

"Edge's, you mean?" Brandt looked up. "I wouldn't say that. Diego must be well over fifty and his wife can't be far behind him. They're not really his contemporaries."

Sophie couldn't help sighing with relief. "Oh, I see. I thought – I imagined they were – younger."

"Because Maria Diego fell in, you mean? Oh, she's a Latin, my dear. Terrifically excitable, some of these women. I expect she got carried away by the catch."

Sophie nodded. "I expect so."

Dinner was over by the time Edge and Piers reappeared, but Violet assured them she hadn't forgotten them. Sophie left Brandt talking to them and joined Rosa in the lounge. Presently Brandt came through, but before they had finished their after-dinner coffee there was the sound of a car cruising down the slope to the house. Brandt clicked his tongue impatiently and Sophie felt sure that he thought it would be Howard Fleming, but when the maid came to the door of the lounge it was to say that Miss Fleming had called.

Janine Fleming came into the room looking dark and exotic in a jungle-printed catsuit, the trousers of which were slit almost to the knee. After greeting Brandt and his sister, she gave Sophie a cool smile and then said: "But where's Edge? I thought he was due back this evening."

Brandt offered her a drink and while he was making it, he said: "He is back. But they were late for dinner. He'll be joining us shortly."

"Oh, I see." Janine looked round and finally chose to sit beside Sophie on the long comfortable couch. "I promised to come over as soon as he got back."

Sophie thought rather bitchily that she hadn't wasted much time, but didn't like to say so. After all, if everyone was honest Janine had more right here than she had.

Edge came in a few minutes later and Janine sprang up to meet him eagerly. "Hello, darling," she murmured silkily. "Have a good trip?"

Edge went to get himself a drink, refusing his aunt's offer of coffee, and Janine accompanied him. They talked together quietly in the corner and presently Edge turned and said that they had decided to go down to Port of Spain for the evening.

"Good idea," exclaimed Brandt with unexpected enthusiasm. "And why don't you take Eve with you? She's had a pretty boring couple of days while both you and Piers have been away. I'm sure she'd enjoy a night out."

Sophie was horrified. "Oh, really," she began, "I'm quite happy staying here –"

"Nonsense!" Brandt seemed determined to provide her with an evening's entertainment. "Piers could go along, too. Make up a foursome."

"Piers has gone to bed," stated Edge flatly. "He was tired. So he won't be going anywhere. But if – Eve – wants to join us . . ."

"No." Sophie was adamant. "No, thank you. I'd – I'd rather not. Besides, I – I have a headache."

Janine was looking undeniably relieved, but Edge seemed sceptical of her pitiful, hackneyed excuse. Brandt sniffed impatiently. "The night air would shift your headache!" he declared.

"No." Sophie shook her head. "Thank you all the same, but no."

Janine breathed more easily. "Well, now that's settled,

116

shall we go?" she asked, obviously eager to get Edge away before his father could make any further suggestions.

Edge inclined his head, swallowing the amber liquid he had poured himself in a gulp. "Why not?" he responded, looking down at her, and Sophie felt a pain like a knife in her stomach.

She went to bed quite early that evening, about ten o'clock, but she couldn't sleep. She kept thinking about Edge and Janine out in the night somewhere, probably in each other's arms, and that prospect was sufficient to banish all thoughts of sleep from her mind. She was beginning to realize that by agreeing to stay on a further two weeks she was making things that much more painful for herself. For it was no use trying to deny it any more, no matter how crazy or irresponsible it might be, she was falling in love with Edge, and there was nothing she could do about it.

CHAPTER SEVEN

TOWARDS midnight Sophie was still wakeful, and with a restless sigh she slid out of bed and put on the cream silk gown which matched her nightdress. She padded to the windows and thrusting open the doors stepped on to the balcony.

The night air was cool and scented, the sound of the sea on the rocks below drifting up to her. She had a sudden longing to be down by the ocean, to feel the salt spray on her face, and know the sense of constancy that only its perpetual movement could give.

Turning back into the room, she trod into low-heeled sandals and opened her bedroom door. The house was silent, only the ticking of clocks disturbing the stillness. Edge hadn't returned home yet, but that didn't concern her. She didn't suppose he would return much before dawn.

Downstairs the mesh door was unlocked and she slipped like a wraith across the terrace and down the stone steps to the courtyard. The garden looked weird and unfamiliar by moonlight, the flamboyant colours of the flowers turned to silver. She was reminded of a poem of Walter de la Mare's she had once read. It had been about moonlight, too, and he had called the poem *Silver*.

The words came back to her as she glided down the steps to the jetty below:

"Slowly, silently, now the moon
Walks the night in her silver shoon;
This way, and that, she peers, and sees
Silver fruit upon silver trees."

It was appropriate somehow, the beautiful words suiting her melancholy mood. His poems had always had the power to invoke in her that sense of unreality and mystery which had been so much a part of her childhood. Escaping from a world peopled by elderly women, the young Sophie had sought solace in stories and poetry, and perhaps it had been that strong sense of make-believe which had first interested her in the theatre. Certainly her formative years had been lonely ones, and living here at Pointe St. Vincente had brought it home to her convincingly how considerable a part of her life had been spent pretending an existence instead of living it.

It was much cooler on the jetty, but after the heat of the day it was welcoming. The water sucked round the base of the rocks throwing up a white-spumed spray that in sunlight glinted rainbow colours. But tonight there was only the moon's luminescence, silvering the waves and casting shadows on the rocks. The sense of isolation that lonely vigil aroused was sufficient to send Sophie back towards the steps again. Her bedroom was at least enclosed in a building where other people were sleeping, but here she might have been the sole survivor of some terrible disaster. Her imagination conjured up tidal waves and hurricanes, and the whistling of the wind that hurried the fleeting clouds across the moon's face became a howling in her ears.

But even as she reached the foot of the steps and started to climb, she heard sounds above. There was no actual engine noise, but the swish of powerful tyres was unmistakable, and presently there was the controlled sound of a car door being closed. Edge must have come back sooner than she had expected.

She paused on the steps, his presence at least banishing the momentary panic she had experienced. She could hardly go up now and confront him. He might think she was checking up on him, and besides, what possible reason could she give for haunting the jetty at this time of night? No, she would have to wait a few minutes and give him time to go to his room before venturing into the house again.

She shivered. The coolness which had been so pleasant when first she came down here had become quite chilling, and her own stupid nerves had created a chill all their own. She found herself wishing she had never left the comparative safety of her bedroom, and even her bed seemed more inviting now.

At last, when she was beginning to feel frozen to the core, she deemed it safe to go up again, and she mounted the stone steps quickly, trying to infuse a little warmth into her body. Even her legs felt stiff and her fingertips were icy.

The house was in darkness and she breathed a sigh of relief. She had had visions of various rooms being illuminated and herself having to crouch down in the bushes and wait for them to be extinguished like some would-be burglar.

She crossed the courtyard and mounted the steps to the terrace. She turned the handle of the mesh door confidently and then stood back, aghast. The door was secured

120

from the inside. She couldn't get in again.

Immediately, the panic which she had felt earlier returned in full force. What was she going to do now? How could she get in without arousing the whole house?

Schooling herself to calmness, she tried to view her position sensibly. Obviously none of the doors were going to be open, but there might conceivably be a window open somewhere. She would have to investigate.

She walked along the terrace and hopefully tried the french doors which opened into the morning room, but they were securely bolted. Further along was the conservatory where they dined on cooler evenings whose long plate glass windows could be slid back on oiled bearings, but that too was secured for the night.

Sophie turned back the other way, passing the mesh door again and climbing several shallow steps to come upon more french doors. These too were locked and she pressed her nose painfully against the glass, trying to see what was beyond. Eventually she recognized it as Brandt's study, and she was about to turn away in despair when a strong hand suddenly caught her arm. She gasped in terror, her imaginings earlier inducing a state of panic-stricken fear, and struggled wildly, but the voice which said: "What the hell do you think you're doing!" was reassuringly familiar.

She slumped, her shoulders sagging, and looked up into Edge's grim face with weary resignation. "I – I – you locked me out," she murmured tremulously.

"Locked you out?" He shook his head uncomprehendingly, and then seemed to become aware of how cold she was as the chilliness of her flesh invaded his fingers even through the cream silk of her gown. "You're frozen!" he muttered savagely. "What in God's name do you think you're doing wandering about outside at this time of night?"

This was clearly a rhetorical question at the moment, because as he spoke he was dragging her after him along the terrace and in through the mesh door. He paused for a moment to secure it again and then walked surefootedly across the darkened hall and into the lounge. Closing the door, he released her to go and switch on a standard lamp, and then turned to face her, a forbidding expression marring his lean good looks.

"Well?" he demanded. "What were you doing?"

Sophie gathered the folds of her robe about her. She was overwhelmingly conscious of the scarcity of her attire compared to his beige suede pants and navy silk shirt, and she wished he would stop staring at her so contemptuously, as if she was something objectionable he had found on his doorstep.

Taking a deep breath, she said: "I went down to the jetty. I – I couldn't sleep, and I felt like – like walking. When – when I came back the door was locked. You must have locked me out."

"Why me?" Edge was imperative.

"Why, because – because –" Sophie hesitated. To say because she had known he wasn't home earlier would be to reveal her awareness of his movements, she realized in dismay. "Well, as – as you're the only person up, it – it had to be you," she finished lamely.

Edge's lips twisted. "Oh, really?"

"In – in any case," she hurried on, trying to distract him, "how did you know it was me?"

Edge lifted his shoulders and let them fall again in a

122

casual gesture. "I didn't. But when one hears someone systematically trying all the doors and windows of the building, one immediately suspects that someone is trying to get in. You'd make no conspirator. You make far too much noise."

Sophie shivered. "Oh, well, thank you for letting me in. I – I think I ought to go back to bed now –"

"You're chilled to the bone. You need something to warm you through or you'll probably catch pneumonia," he exclaimed impatiently. "You'd better have a drink."

"Oh, no, really." Sophie shook her head. "I'll be all right once I get between the sheets –"

"But I insist," said Edge, in a tone that brooked no argument, and Sophie quivered but made no further protest.

He poured a generous measure of brandy into a goblet and brought it across to her, watching her as she sipped the fiery liquid. She was holding the folds of her cream gown closely at the neck with one hand and gripping the glass with the other, and she was supremely conscious of her vulnerability where he was concerned. She wished he would go and get himself a drink or do something other than stand before her, compelling her to examine every inch of his shirt-front, opened at the neck to reveal the smooth column of his throat. Her gaze travelled down to his thigh muscles straining against the close-fitting suede of his trousers, to the suede boots on his feet. She had an almost overpowering urge to move closer to him, to discover his reaction if she did so, but common sense prevailed.

"Do you feel better now?" His voice broke into her musings and she looked up nervously.

"Oh – oh, yes, thank you." There was still some of the brandy left in the goblet. "I'm sorry to have been such a – a nuisance."

Edge's eyes narrowed. "You should tell people when you intend taking midnight strolls. I might not have been around to let you in, or you might, conceivably, have had an accident."

"What do you mean?"

"Those steps can be dangerous, especially at night. You could have tripped, or twisted your ankle. Then what would you have done?"

"I don't know." Sophie held out the goblet. "I don't want any more, thank you."

"Finish it!"

"No. I – I'm not all that keen on it."

"You aren't meant to like it," he commented dryly. "It's medicine, and you know what they say about medicine."

Sophie drew a shaking breath. "I really can't swallow any more."

Edge looked at her intently, and then, deliberately it seemed, his gaze dropped the length of her silk-clad body, returning to rest for a moment on her slightly parted lips.

"Tell me," he said, and she sensed a self-contempt within him for voicing such a question, "isn't there some young man back in London waiting impatiently for your return?"

Sophie took a backward step. "I don't – see that it's any business of yours," she answered, rather unevenly.

Edge covered the small distance she had put between them with indolent grace. "But I'm interested," he remarked, and the amber eyes glittered rather unnervingly.

Sophie took another step backward, looking round desperately for somewhere to put the brandy goblet. "This is a ridiculous conversation to be having at one o'clock in the morning," she protested.

"Then answer the question." Edge was impatient.

Sophie took another step backward and came up against a carved Regency chair which stood to one side of the doors. "Will you please stop baiting me, and allow me to go to bed?" she appealed, her fingers in danger of separating the stem of the goblet from its bowl.

"I'm not baiting you." Edge had halted in front of her, only several inches between them. Unhurriedly, he put out a hand and tugged rather cruelly at a strand of her hair. "I want to know. My father tells me you've agreed to stay on for another two weeks, and I'm curious to know why."

"Oh, I see." Sophie tried to slow her quickened breathing. "Well – well, you must know why I'm staying. I – I've grown fond of – of Brandt and Piers – and – and I like it here."

Edge's lids lowered, his attention appearing to be concentrated on her fingers plucking revealingly at the neckline of her gown. "I notice my name is conspicuous by its absence from that small group of people you're fond of," he remarked huskily.

Sophie trembled. "I – I shouldn't have thought that would worry you," she managed, with an attempt at lightness. "There – there seem to be plenty of people more than fond of you as it is."

His lids lifted slightly and he looked at her intently. "And how do you know that? I may be distinctly underloved."

125

"I doubt it." Sophie glanced away from him. "Oh, please – let me go!"

Edge studied her troubled countenance with a disturbing expression on his face. "You don't make a very good accomplice, do you, Eve?"

Her eyes darted back to his. "I don't know what you mean."

"Don't you?" He cupped her neck between his fingers, and she almost jumped out of her skin. "Relax. I'm not going to hurt you."

"Let – let go of me!"

"And if I don't? What will you do? Call for help?"

"*Please!*" Sophie had reached the point of being prepared to plead with him. "I'm tired. I want to go to bed."

His fingers explored the nape of her neck under her hair, probing the neckline of her gown. She stood rigid under his hands, hardly able to breathe, so shocked she could scarcely think, let alone anything else.

"Such soft skin," he murmured, a little hoarsely. "For God's sake, stop holding yourself so stiffly. I've told you, I won't hurt you."

"Edge –" There was a break in her voice now, and he looked away from what he was doing and into her eyes. She felt him propelling her towards him, she felt the muscles of his legs through the thin silk of her gown, and his hands sliding over her shoulders and down to her hips. She wanted to resist, she knew she ought to resist, but her body moulded itself to his almost without volition, and there was nothing but his warmth and hardness, and the clean male smell of him. And then the brandy goblet was crushed from her fingers to fall and break fragmentarily against the cool tiling of the floor, splashing her bare feet

126

with its erstwhile contents and startling her into awareness of what she was doing.

She caught her breath. "The glass –" she began, but he was bending his head towards her, his mouth frankly sensuous.

"To hell with the glass!" he muttered, his mouth burning against the curve of her throat. "Damn you, don't stiffen up on me again."

Sophie twisted her head from side to side in a vain attempt to escape the inevitable, but with a muffled imprecation he lifted one hand and caught her head, imprisoning it until his mouth had fastened itself to hers. For a brief moment she tried to speak, to protest, but he was too strong for her, and her lips softened into willing response. He released her head and gathered her closer against him, his kiss hardening and lengthening into passion. Inexperienced as she was, Sophie nevertheless understood the demanding urgency behind that kiss, but while sanity urged her to fight him, a deeper, more fundamental need made her slide her arms around his waist, uncaring any longer about the deep *décolleté* of her attire.

But now Edge put his hands behind his back, wrenching her arms from around him, trying to push her roughly away from him. Sophie, however, was still very much the victim of her own newly awakened senses, and when he attempted to draw back she went after him, clinging to him, raising her mouth to his appealingly. She heard his savagely-drawn breath through the mists of desire, but then his mouth was on hers again, and she was content.

"No," he groaned at last, when he eventually lifted his head. "Dear God, *no!*"

"Edge?" she breathed questioningly, her soft lips parted, her hair a tangled glory of gold about her bemused face. "Edge – don't push me away."

Edge gritted his teeth, and taking her by the shoulders shook her so violently that her teeth chattered and her head lolled helplessly on her slender neck. But the brutal action had the desired effect, and she blinked her eyes rapidly, staring at him in dawning comprehension. Shame caused the hot colour to flood her cheeks, and her hands sought her throat, gathering the folds of silk together with trembling fingers.

"It's a bit late for that, isn't it?" Edge asked, unpleasantly, turning away, his own self-contempt evident. "My God, just get out of my sight, Sophie!"

For a moment Sophie couldn't grasp his whole meaning, but then that final word he had used got through to her. "S – Sophie?" She almost choked. "You – you know my name!"

Edge walked to the drinks tray and poured himself a stiff Scotch, swallowing it before replying. Then he poured another and turned to rest against the table, his expression cold and forbidding. "I've known your name ever since you arrived here," he stated bleakly. "Now, get out of here before I do something we'd both regret."

Sophie couldn't take it in, not all at once. Too much had happened in too brief a time for her to absorb the implications completely. She moved her head slowly from side to side, trying to assimilate what all this meant to her, but when she looked at Edge her eyes dropped before the naked hatred she saw burning in his.

"Oh, Edge –" she began appealingly, unable to accept that the man who had been making love to her so passion-ately a few minutes ago could have changed so dramatically, but he cut her short, his tone incisive.

"I don't want to talk to you any more," he muttered, wiping his mouth with the back of his hand. "Just go away and leave me alone!"

He turned his back on her and poured himself another Scotch. Sophie took a tentative step towards the door and then halted. Her brain was buzzing chaotically and there was an awful feeling of sickness in her stomach, and yet she couldn't believe Edge had suddenly shed all feeling for her.

But thinking of those moments when she had been in his arms brought another wave of self-condemnation. What must he be thinking of her, even aside from the despicable deception she had been a party to? What kind of a woman did he think she was, responding to him in that wholly wanton way, practically begging him to make love to her? Did he imagine she was used to allowing a man to hold her so intimately that every inch of her body tingled from the pressure of his?

"Edge, please!" she whispered. "Let me explain!"

"*Get out!*"

There was such a wealth of disgust in his voice then that she went, stumbling from the room blindly, making her way up the winding wrought iron staircase as silently as the racking sobs which rose up inside her would allow.

It was an amazing thing that no matter what the night had held the morning always dawned with bright inconsequence. For Sophie, roused from a drugged sleep by the maid, Liza, the brilliance of the day was like a mocking salute to her misery. She struggled up in the big

129

bed, blinking disbelievingly at the small clock on the bedside table. *Eleven o'clock!* It couldn't be so late!

The maid held a tray on which reposed a jug of coffee and some warm rolls. "Miss Violet, she said you'd be wanting this," she intoned, her expression vaguely sullen. Sophie was sure she had never really forgiven her for unwittingly causing Violet to speak harshly to her.

"Oh! Well, thank you." Sophie scrambled across the bed to push aside some things on the bedside table, makin room for Liza to put down the tray. "I – I'll get up at once."

Liza shrugged. "Is that all?"

Sophie sighed. "Yes, thank you."

Liza shrugged again and left the room, and after she had gone, Sophie slumped, bending her head dejectedly, her hair falling in a heavy curtain about her face. She rested her head in her hands and heaved a heavy sigh, wondering whether Edge thought she had remained in bed deliberately to avoid the inevitable. Of course, he would be bound to think so. He couldn't know that she had lain awake for hours after she left him, sick and miserable, eventually swallowing half a dozen aspirins to find oblivion in unconsciousness.

She didn't touch the rolls, but the coffee was welcome. Her mouth felt terrible, and after gulping some of the steaming liquid she went into the bathroom and cleaned her teeth. Her reflection in the mirror was not inspiring. Her eyes looked dark and shadowed from hours of weeping, and her cheeks were pale and drawn.

Eventually she took a shower, a cold one, hoping the sharpness of the water would tone up her skin. Indeed, she did feel better when she emerged, but the hollow sensation in her stomach could not be banished by physical means.

She dressed in pink hipster jeans and a navy tank top, brushing her hair with brisk, painful strokes. She would not be a mouse, she thought, cowering in a corner, waiting for the axe to strike. She would go out and meet it, as courageously as she could, and show Edge she was no coward whatever else she might be.

Downstairs, she encountered Piers in the hall, and her nerves tautened at the resemblance between him and his father.

"Well, hi!" he greeted her mockingly. "This is a fine time to be getting up. I've been hanging about for hours waiting for you."

Sophie's eyes were guarded. "For me? Why?"

Piers raised his eyes heavenward in obvious exaspera-tion. "Why? She asks me – why?" He shook his head. "Don't we usually go swimming together in the morn-ings? I mean, I know I've been away for a couple of days, but that's no reason to assume the situation has suddenly changed."

"Oh!" Sophie pressed her palms together. "I – I for-got."

"You forgot? How could you forget such an import-ant engagement?" Piers was pretending to be hurt. "So what are you waiting for? Don't you want to go swim-ming?"

Sophie hesitated, running her tongue over her upper lip, nervously waiting for Edge or his father to hear their voices and appear. "I – I – I don't much feel like swim-ming today," she said at last.

Piers stepped forward, examining her features more

closely. "Say, are you okay?" he asked with concern. "You're looking sort of pale and wan. Did you have a late night?"

"You could say that." Sophie managed a faint smile. "I – I didn't sleep very well."

"No, I can see that," Piers nodded. "Come on, let's go and sit on the terrace. I'll tell you all about our trip, shall I?"

Sophie still hesitated. "Er – where's Brandt – and – and your father?"

Piers grimaced good-naturedly. "Why? What do you want them for? Isn't my company good enough?"

"Oh, Piers, of course it is." Sophie was contrite. "It's just that – well, the house seems quiet, that's all."

Piers shrugged. "They've driven down to Port Maguerre, actually. Brandt wanted to take you along, but you were asleep, and Dad said you'd find it all pretty boring anyway."

Sophie felt weak with reaction and relief. "Wh – where is Port Maguerre?" she asked faintly.

"South side of the island. Near the oil fields."

"Oh, I see." Sophie swayed suddenly and Piers caught her wrists to support her.

"Say, you're really not well, are you?" he exclaimed. "Come on. We'll just take it easy today. I'll have Violet bring us some coffee on to the terrace."

But Sophie was determinedly pulling herself together. Obviously Edge had said nothing as yet, but how long could she expect those circumstances to last? She had to think sanely and sensibly, and the sooner she sent that cable to Eve advising her of what had happened, the better.

132

Sitting on the terrace with Piers, eating some of Violet's home-made ginger biscuits and drinking a cup of strong black coffee she began to feel almost herself again. Cradling her coffee cup in her hands, she decided that nothing had outwardly changed at all. Edge had said that he had known all along who she was, and therefore her position in the household, so far as she was concerned, was no more precipitous now than it had been before. Except that now she knew that she might be exposed at any moment . . .

Allowing her brain to work again brought her back to the inescapable puzzle of how Edge had known she was not Eve all along. That and the reasons behind his not exposing her had been partially responsible for her insomnia the night before, and thinking of these things brought back the sick feeling of despair to her stomach.

Taking a sip of her coffee, she deliberately turned her mind to other things. Looking across at Piers, she said quietly: "Do you think we could go into Port of Spain today?"

"Port of Spain?" Piers stared at her. "Now, do you think that's a good idea when you've been feeling so lousy?"

Sophie forced a smile. "Oh, I'm all right now. I guess I got too much sun yesterday, that's all."

Piers looked doubtful. "Even so . . . What do you want in Port of Spain? I could get Joseph to go in for you."

Sophie sighed. "No, I – I'd rather do it myself. Besides, I haven't really seen much of the place at all. I thought we might do some sightseeing."

"And you want to go shopping?"

Sophie bit her lip. "I want to send a cable, actually."

"A cable?" Piers raised his eyebrows. "To anyone I know?"

"No. Just to a friend back home. Birthday greetings. You know the sort of thing."

She had decided to admit sending a cable to Piers because she would need his help in finding the office.

Piers finished his coffee and thrust his cup aside. "So when do you want to go?"

"Whenever you like."

"Right now?"

"That would be marvellous!"

"Okay." Piers studied her pale cheeks thoughtfully. "And if you begin to feel unwell you tell me, right?"

"Right." Sophie got to her feet. "Thanks, Piers. You're a darling!"

"Am I?" Piers gave her an old-fashioned look. "So how come we never get any further than holding hands? We are kissin' kin, you know."

Sophie had to laugh at this. "I think I'd better get my sunglasses," she remarked, backing towards the french doors, and then turned away with a twinge of pain as she recalled the way she had backed away from Edge only the night before.

They went to Port of Spain in the estate car Brandt had first shown her the estate in. Piers was an excellent driver, and when he explained that his father had taught him to drive on St. Vincente land before he was eight years old, Sophie could understand why.

"Do – do you remember your mother?" she asked tentatively, unable to banish thoughts of Edge completely from her mind.

Piers glanced sideways at her. "Do you realize that's

the first time you've asked me about my mother?"

Sophie made a dismissing gesture with her hands. "Is it? Well, I suppose I didn't want to sound as though I was prying."

"Why not? She was your aunt."

"Yes, well . . ." Sophie traced the pattern of the leather upholstery with her nail. "It's nothing to do with me really, is it?"

"I suppose not." Piers swung the wheel to avoid a black-skinned child playing by the roadside. "Oh, yes, I remember her. I was, I suppose, about seven when she died. But she wasn't the be-all and end-all of my existence at that time. I guess Violet was more of a mother to me than she was."

"You always lived here, then?"

"At Pointe St. Vincente? Oh, yes. You see, my father was working for Brandt and – well, it's such a big house. Brandt wouldn't have cared to live alone."

"There was Rosa."

"Yes, but you've met Rosa. She's never entirely with us, surely you've noticed? And in any case, after your mother ran away I think Brandt didn't want to risk my father getting any ideas like that."

Sophie nodded. "I suppose – I suppose your father was very – upset – when she died?"

Piers assumed a thoughtful expression. "I guess he was in some ways."

"What do you mean?" Sophie's brows drew together.

Piers gave a wry grimace. "Well, my mother wasn't like him. I don't honestly know why he married her." Then he sighed. "Dammit, yes, I do. She told him she was pregnant and he did the decent thing!"

135

"Oh!" Sophie swung round in her seat, her heart hammering heavily. "But I suppose he was happy when you were born?"

"Sort of. But as I was born approximately a year later, things weren't exactly blissful between them."

Sophie was horrified. "You mean – you mean –"

"Yes, that's right. The oldest trick in the book, and he fell for it. What else could he do? The St. Vincentes are an old-established family. They have an old-fashioned idea of honour. It would have been inconceivable for my father to deny responsibility even while he suspected it wasn't true."

Sophie shook her head. "How awful!"

"Yes, wasn't it?" Piers sounded bored by the whole affair. "But that's life, as they say."

Sophie couldn't leave it alone now. "But afterwards – after you were born, surely things improved then?"

"Not really. You see, my mother wanted to be married, but that was as far as her imagination took her. When she had to cope with the responsibilities of a husband and family, she took to her bed."

"You can't be serious! Who told you all this?"

"What do you think? That my father regaled me with his side of the story and alienated my mother's affections? I didn't need to be told, Eve. I was there. I saw it happening."

"But you couldn't have. You were too young."

"Initially, yes, but children begin to notice things pretty quickly."

"Was your mother ill then?"

"I don't think she ever really got over having me. At least, it was convenient for her to pretend so. And you see, your mother had died in childbirth and I guess both my father and Brandt were programmed to react the way they did. I don't believe she was ever a real wife to my father afterwards. And of course, she did develop cancer, and then . . ." He shrugged. "Maybe I sound callous. I'm not really. It's just that – well, she was never a real mother to me either. If I took my bruised knees or bleeding head to her she'd practically throw a faint, and I got used to going to Violet and being comforted by her. She was my real mother. People think that blood ties are everything. I don't. People can share the same blood and hate one another. Violet mothered me, and that's what being a parent is all about, isn't it?"

"I suppose so." Sophie was absorbed with what he had told her, it explained why Geraldine's name was so seldom mentioned; why Piers and his father were so close.

The telegraph office was in Independence Square, renamed, Piers told her, when independence was granted in 1962. There were a number of beautiful parks and squares awaiting exploration, but right now Sophie had only one thing on her mind.

To her relief, Piers agreed to hang about outside while she went in and wrote out her message to Eve. It seemed terribly long when she had finished, but she needed to know what kind of a deal Eve had tried to make with her grandfather and would definitely not make through her, and also Eve had to be informed that her uncle was aware of Sophie's identity. When she eventually emerged after paying the clerk what seemed like an enormous sum of money, she found Piers kicking his heels impatiently.

"For heaven's sake!" he exclaimed, when he saw her. "What kind of birthday greetings were those? Do you realize I've been waiting here nearly half an hour?"

"I'm sorry, Piers." Sophie was apologetic. "But you know how it is. I'm not used to sending cables."

Piers gave her a wry stare. "Really? And I suppose you didn't mention that you were staying on here another two weeks, did you?"

Sophie frowned. "I – I might have done."

Piers nodded. "I thought so. This friend whose birthday it is – it's a man, isn't it?"

Sophie opened her mouth to deny that statement and then closed it again. At least if the fact that she had sent a cable became public knowledge Edge would not start putting two and two together if Piers told him the cable had been sent to a man. Shrugging her shoulders, she said slowly: "I have friends of both sexes, and I don't see that it matters either way."

Piers had the grace to look slightly shamefaced at this. "I guess not. I'm just fed up with waiting, that's all. Come on. We'll go get some lunch and then I'll show you a little of our capital city."

It was a relaxing afternoon. For a short time Sophie managed to push her own anxieties to the back of her mind, determining not to live in an agony of anticipation when there was nothing she could do to change things. Instead, she shared Piers' delight in being a tourist in one of the most attractive cities in the world. They meandered along Frederick Street, that most cosmopolitan of shopping thoroughfares, and she couldn't resist buying herself a white silk caftan edged with the most intricate hand embroidery in shades of red, blue and green. At least she would have something to remind herself of this interlude in her life, she thought, and the despair was hard to keep at bay.

Afterwards they took one of the small, decorated carts that plied their trade along Charlotte Street where the market spread its untidy mess of produce over the pavements, and visited the harbour where tourist vessels were berthed en route for South America and the other islands along the archipelago. It was pleasant to sit in the shade of the awning and watch the hectic life of the city pass one by, but when they finally returned to where Piers had left the estate car Sophie felt a tremendous sense of regret. The day was almost over and now she had to go back and face whatever was ahead of her.

They arrived back at Pointe St. Vincente at about six o'clock and Sophie saw at once that Edge and Brandt must be home, too. The limousine Edge invariably drove was parked on the courtyard, its windows wide, the bonnet still warm.

"Dad's back," remarked Piers, unnecessarily. "Come on! We might just be in time for some tea. I could surely use some."

Sophie followed him up the steps rather more slowly. She dreaded the moment when she would have to encounter Edge again, and see the hard mockery in his eyes. She dreaded reading the contempt in his face and knowing that he must regard her with active dislike. If only she had never taken that walk last evening. If only the scene in the lounge had never happened . . .

They entered the hall. It was cool after the heat outside, the scent of roses from an enormous bowl on a tall pedestal filling the air with their heady fragrance. Sophie paused to admire them, anything to delay the evil moment, and was bent towards them when Edge came down

139

the steps which led to his father's study. He was not alone. There was a girl following him and for a moment Sophie supposed it was Janine and turned away. But then he spoke, and his words shocked her into immobility.

"Ah, you're back!" he remarked with cool nonchalance. "I'm so glad, Eve, because you've a visitor – from England. Isn't that amazing? A Miss Sophie Slater!"

For a moment Sophie really thought she was going to faint there at his feet. Her legs went weak at the knees and a mist came before her eyes. But then Eve, for that was who it amazingly was, came forward, tugging her arm rather impatiently and saying:

"Darling, don't look so shocked! I know it's a surprise, but you know how I adore surprising people!"

CHAPTER EIGHT

SOPHIE sat in the wrought iron bathroom chair with its patterned orange and cream cushion and watched Eve soaping herself liberally in the cream and apricot luxury of the facilities which had been provided for Sophie's sole use. Eve had filled the bath with bubbles and was now wallowing lazily, indifferent to the anxious expression on her friend's face.

"Darling, what you seem to be missing is the fact that Edge can't expose you now," she stated calmly, flicking a small speck of foam towards the other girl.

"Why?" asked Sophie, her mouth working. "Why?"

"Darling, if he had been going to do that he'd have done it a couple of weeks ago. Don't you see? He's made himself an accessory."

Sophie dug her nail into the metal arm of the chair. "You make it sound so simple!"

"Well, it is, isn't it? I mean, it's rather a bizarre situation, isn't it? You playing me – and me playing you!"

"It's ridiculous!" Sophie got abruptly to her feet. "Eve, you've got to let me out of this. Tell your grandfather who you are and I'll go home –"

"No!"

"Why not?"

"Well, don't you see? That would be stupid now. It's obvious from the way he talks of you that he regards you with real affection. It would be cruel to tell him the truth."

Sophie turned on her angrily. "Don't you mean – it

wouldn't be politic?"

Eve narrowed her eyes. "What did you say?"

"You heard me. There's more to this charade than a desire to placate an old man. You sent me here because you wanted something, but you omitted to tell me what!"

Eve stood up and reached for a fleecy white towel. "Sophie, don't get so heated about everything! I always imagined you to be a calm, sensible girl. Suddenly you seem to have developed entirely different characteristics. I wonder why?"

"Oh, don't be silly, Eve!" Sophie stared at her frustratedly. "Look, I did what you wanted. I came here. Don't you think I deserve some kind of an explanation?"

"Perhaps you do, perhaps you don't." Eve was annoyingly ambiguous. "Look, darling, can you lend me some clean undies? My things are still at the hotel. It's just until Joseph collects my case."

Sophie clenched her fists. "You can't mean to stay here!"

"Why not? It's much more comfortable than a hotel."

"But Edge knows – I mean, he's got to realize who you are."

"So what? It adds a sort of piquancy to the occasion, don't you think?"

Sophie heaved a sigh. "But what about John Fellowes? I imagined you'd be in the Middle East by now."

Eve stepped delicately out of the towel. "Darling, what about those undies? I can't stand here in the nude indefinitely."

Sophie uttered an impatient exclamation, but turned and went obediently into her bedroom and rummaging through a drawer came back with what the other girl wanted. Then, as she was fastening the straps of her bra, Sophie went on: "The Middle East, Eve? What happened to that trip that prevented you from coming out here?"

Eve stepped back into the slim-fitting navy shift she had worn to come to Pointe St. Vincente and turned for Sophie to zip her up. Then she said: "There was no Middle East trip, Sophie. I made it up. But there will be – with your assistance."

"What do you mean?" Sophie was astounded.

"Oh, Sophie, do I have to explain right now? Couldn't we just sit and have a cigarette and talk about what kind of a time you've had? Aside from my uncle's revelations, you have enjoyed it, haven't you? And Piers seems a honey."

Sophie marched back into the bathroom to empty the bath and Eve came negligently to the open door. "Darling, don't be like this. Can't we at least talk civilly together?"

Sophie stood up. "How can you stand there and expect me to condone your behaviour? I – I think you've behaved despicably, if you want to know!"

Eve shrugged. "You agreed to come here, Sophie," she pointed out dryly.

"I know I did, and I've regretted it ever since." Sophie brushed past her into the bedroom. "I'm not cut out for intrigue, Eve. If you're not about to tell me right now what all this is about, I'm going to go down there and tell Brandt everything. Do you understand? *Everything!*"

Eve regarded the other girl thoughtfully. "I don't believe you, darling. But if you insist . . ."

"I do." Sophie was adamant.

"All right." Eve shrugged and reaching for her handbag which she had dropped carelessly on to the bed she drew out her cigarettes. Once one was lit, she dropped elegantly down into a basketwork chair and inhaled deeply. "Now, where shall I begin?"

"At the beginning," advised Sophie shortly.

"Oh, yes. That would be when my father died. Well, as you know, I wrote to my grandfather then and told him what had happened, and as you also know, he was very sympathetic. We corresponded, he suggested I came out to Trinidad, and I stalled."

"Why?"

Eve studied the glowing tip of her cigarette. "I hate to admit this, but I'm in love with John Fellowes."

Sophie blinked. "In love with him?" she echoed.

"Yes." Eve gave a casual movement of her shoulders. "I never thought any man would mean that much to me ..." She snapped her fingers. "But John does."

"So where's the problem?" Sophie was curious.

"Well, just because I've admitted that I'm in love with John Fellowes it doesn't presuppose that he's in love with me. On the contrary, I doubt if he even knows that I exist."

Sophie gave her a wry look. "Come off it, Eve. You're not the type of woman to let herself go unnoticed for long."

"Thank you, Sophie." Eve gave a small, secretive smile. "I'll take that as a compliment. Nevertheless, in spite of what you say, John Fellowes hasn't got where he is today without having an eye to the main chance. He knows where he wants to go and he's going to get there. Journalism is okay, it's interesting, but it can be damn dangerous on these overseas assignments, and he knows where the money lies. It's in television, it's in becoming a personality, someone whose name is instantly recognizable, and that's why he wants to make this series of documentaries."

"You mean the idea of this Middle Eastern assignment was feasible?"

"Not only feasible, it's imperative. At least, from John's point of view. Don't you see – if I could provide the money, he'd take me with him!"

"Oh, Eve!" Sophie stared at her in disbelief. "You can't seriously mean this!"

"Why not?"

"Well – well, because – even if it's true, even if this Fellowes man does need a backer and you provide him with one, that wouldn't necessarily mean that he'd become interested in you! Heavens, I'd say it could work in exactly the opposite way. He could become famous, pay you back what he's borrowed, and drop you like a hot potato!"

Eve's lips twisted impatiently. "Yes, well, your simple reasoning would come up with something like that, wouldn't it? You don't imagine I'd be foolish enough to hand over the money without any guarantees, do you? I'm not stupid, you know."

Sophie shook her head. "And that's what all this is about? An opportunity to cheat an old man out of several thousand pounds?"

Eve gave the younger girl an exasperated stare. "I'm not cheating anybody out of anything. It's my right. I'm my mother's only surviving relative. Half of everything here should be mine!"

Sophie gasped. "You forget – your mother gave everything up when she married your father. Besides, I always thought the son inherited everything."

"Edge, you mean?" Eve's eyes flickered. "Tell me: exactly how did he come to reveal that he knew who you were?"

Sophie was the one to look uncomfortable then. "Does it matter? He told me, that's enough."

"Is it?" Eve studied her thoughtfully, noting the sudden darkening of colour in Sophie's cheeks. "Ah, yes, I'm beginning to understand. He's quite a dish, isn't he? Uncle Edge. And so long as he thought you were his niece there was nothing doing –"

"It was nothing like that!" Sophie was horrified. "I've told you. He's known from the beginning."

"How?"

"I don't know." Sophie turned away. "Eve, for goodness' sake, stop trying to shift the blame on to my shoulders."

Eve pressed out the remains of her cigarette in the ashtray. "I'm not blaming you. In your shoes, I'd have probably done the same. Tell me – what is he like? Edge, I mean."

Sophie gasped, looking back at her over her shoulder. "That's a foul thing to say!"

"Why is it? Oh, Sophie, you're as transparent as water. It's obvious that you've noticed him. But has he noticed you, I wonder?"

"Eve, please! We're not discussing me. We're discussing you – and your position here. Look, let me go back. You can tell them what you like. You can pretend you came with an urgent message from the paper – anything. Just so long as I can go back."

"No."

146

"But why? Eve, I've been very patient. You've lied to me. You pretended your grandfather didn't know you worked for a newspaper; you pretended he was old and senile, in danger of imminent death; you sent me here totally unaware of the real reasons behind this visit! How can you expect to keep me here now?"

Eve rose to her feet. "If you go now everything will be ruined. Can't you see that? My grandfather will never forgive me if he learns that I sent you in my place."

"And do you honestly think Edge will allow him to advance you money knowing that you hadn't even the decency to come here yourself?"

"He might. If the terms were acceptable."

"What terms?"

"Well, for instance, there's the question of why he didn't expose you as an impostor in the first place. Do you think that could have a more personal significance?"

"Whatever are you talking about?"

"I'm talking about you and Edge. Do you think he's attracted to you?"

Sophie caught her breath. "No! No, of course not."

"It's a possibility."

"You're not really trying to tell me that Edge didn't tell his father who I was because he found me attractive! Oh, Eve, don't be so ridiculous!"

"What's ridiculous about it? What reasons did he give for not revealing who you were?"

"He – he didn't give a reason."

"There you are, then."

"Oh, Eve! If only you knew how wrong you are! Edge isn't attracted to me. He – he hates the sight of me. He told me so."

147

"Really?" Eve looked intrigued. "Curiouser and curiouser, as Alice said. Well, he has to have a reason for not exposing you, and it's up to us to find out what that reason is and use it to our best advantage."

Sophie shook her head vigorously. "You can do what you like, Eve, but don't involve me."

"What? Would you have my grandfather find out the truth without any preparation? How do you think he'd take it? It might be quite a shock."

Sophie moved restlessly. "He has to know sooner or later."

"Why? Why shouldn't our original plan work?"

"*Your* original plan," Sophie corrected her grimly.

"All right, my plan." Eve nodded. "If you'd stop behaving like a temperamental ballerina you'd see that nothing's changed. Everything can go on as before except that now you'll have me to support you."

"No." Sophie pressed her palms to her cheeks. "No. I won't do it."

"What will you do, then? Expose yourself? Because I don't intend to do it, and somehow I don't think Edge will either."

Sophie paced about the room. "My God," she said, "what a situation!" Then a thought struck her. "But if you weren't going abroad with John Fellowes, why did you send me here? Why couldn't you have come yourself? Why are you here now?"

"Like I told you, darling. The idea of playing the prodigal granddaughter didn't appeal to me. It still doesn't. You're much more the sort of granddaughter my grandfather would expect to have."

"You're completely unscrupulous, aren't you?" exclaimed Sophie, halting before her and looking her squarely in the face. "How dare you attempt to manipulate people to your own ends and expect to get away with it?"

"Oh, really, Sophie, don't be childish! What have I done that's so terrible, after all? You've made my grandfather very happy. Much happier, I'm sure, than I could have made him –"

"And you think that excuses you? Because of your selfishness I've made your grandfather happy? Eve, there's more than that to take into consideration."

"I might have known your bourgeois conscience would start troubling you," commented Eve maliciously.

"Start?" echoed Sophie tremulously. "It's never stopped troubling me!"

"You mean you haven't enjoyed yourself here? That there hasn't been any occasion when you haven't been wishing yourself back home?"

Sophie had to be honest. "No, I didn't say that exactly –"

"There you are, then –"

"*No!*" Sophie was desperate. "Eve – please –"

But suddenly, before Eve could reply, they heard a loud altercation going on just outside Sophie's bedroom door, and both girls turned to stare at the door uncomprehendingly. Sophie's heart pounded, but she moved to open it, standing back in confusion when the housekeeper, Violet, came into the room.

"I'm sorry about that, Miss Eve!" she addressed herself apologetically to Sophie. "But I caught that girl Liza listening at your door."

Sophie caught at the door handle for support. "Liza?"

"Yes'm. I sent her along here almost ten minutes ago to tell your friend here, Miss Slater, that her room was ready and waiting for her. Of course, when she didn't come back, I came to see what was going on, and I caught her just standing here – listening!"

Sophie let go of the door and sank down weakly on to the bed. "I – I see." She looked across at Eve and the other girl moved quickly forward.

"I trust you'll see that she's severely reprimanded," she exclaimed, and Sophie marvelled at the coolness of her tone. "One can't have that sort of thing going on. Has it happened before?"

Violet responded automatically to the authority in Eve's voice. "Not that I know of, Miss Slater. But don't you worry, I'll speak to Mr. Brandt about her. She's an insolent girl and perhaps it might be as well if she were to seek other employment."

Eve breathed more easily. "I think that's a very good idea, Violet," she remarked, with a smile. "After all, you have your guests' well-being to think of, haven't you? And all this reflects on you, doesn't it?"

Violet nodded, smoothing her apron. "Leave it to me, miss."

"Good." Eve bent and picked up her handbag giving Sophie a pointed look. "And now will you show me my room? I'm rather tired. Do you think it would be possible for me to have dinner in my room this evening? I'm sure – Miss Eve – could make my apologies for me."

Sophie hadn't time to protest before Eve moved out of the door with the housekeeper and she could hear Violet assuring her warmly that it would be no trouble at all. But after the door had closed behind them Sophie buried her face in her hands, shaking uncontrollably. It was all very well for Eve to behave so calmly, but she hadn't lived here, she didn't know these people; when the crunch came she would not have to bear the brunt of knowing that she had inspired an affection in Brandt and Piers which was entirely unwarranted.

Sophie delayed going down for dinner until the very last moment and appeared at the moment the maid had come to tell Brandt that it was ready. This evening all the family were dining at home, and Brandt looked rather perturbed when Sophie hastily explained that her friend was too tired to come down to dinner.

"She's not ill, is she?" he asked frowningly. "She seemed perfectly well earlier on."

Sophie shook her head, avoiding Edge's sardonic gaze. "No, she's not ill. Just tired. You know how it is? Travelling from England and everything."

"Oh, but she told us she had been here a few days and just decided to look you up on the spur of the moment," observed Edge mockingly, as they all seated themselves at the table in the conservatory.

Sophie flushed. "Oh, really? Well, I expect she's been doing quite a bit of travelling about since she got here."

Brandt stared at his son. "I don't recall Miss Slater saying when she arrived in Trinidad."

Edge shrugged. "Didn't she? I must have been mistaken."

Sophie cast an angry glance in his direction. "Everyone makes mistakes sometimes."

"Yes, they do, don't they?" Edge's tongue had a sharpness to it now. "But some make more than others."

Brandt frowned at his son. "Don't take any notice of

Edge, my dear," he advised kindly. "He's in rather a bad humour, I'm afraid."

"You don't need to make excuses for me, Brandt!"

"Don't I?" Brandt looked away from him, seeking Sophie's concerned face. "I'm afraid our day at Port Maguerre was not an unqualified success. A fault has developed in the pipeline from our well at Augustina, and Edge spent the best part of our time there crawling over machinery. And the puncture we developed on the way home didn't help. It's just as well you weren't with us, Eve. I'd not have cared for you to hear the language."

Sophie managed a relieved smile. "Piers took me to Port of Spain."

"Yes, so I hear." Brandt looked at his grandson. "You're very quiet this evening. Is something wrong?"

Piers looked up from the prawn cocktail the maid had set before him. "What? Oh, no." He shook his head. "I was thinking, that's all."

Sophie looked at him swiftly. Did Piers know anything? Now that Eve was here had Edge decided to reveal Sophie's identity to his son? After all, it was Eve who was Piers' cousin, Eve who was Edge's niece.

Piers caught her worried look and smiled at her. "How do you feel now?" he asked. Then to the table in general, he added: "Eve wasn't very well this morning. I was loath to take her sightseeing, but she insisted."

"What was wrong?" Brandt was concerned. "Of course, you said you had a headache yesterday evening when I suggested you went out with Edge and Janine."

"It was nothing." Sophie tackled a prawn without much appetite. "Just too much sun, I should think."

"It can be dangerous," Brandt agreed. "You must take

152

more care. We wouldn't want you to be ill and miss the carnival next week."

"Is it carnival time again?" Rosa shook her head a trifle bemusedly. "How the years pass by! It seems no time at all since your mother was preparing for the carnival."

"Yes, well, that's all in the past," commented Brandt dryly.

Rosa seemed not to hear him as she went on: "That was when your mother ran away, you know. At carnival time. They weren't missed, you see, not for hours."

"That will do, Rosa!" Brandt's voice was harsher now, and it seemed to penetrate his sister's reverie. She looked along at him in pained silence and for a few minutes conversation lapsed.

When the meal was over, Sophie would have retired to her room, but Edge prevented her. "I'd like to talk to you – Eve!" he remarked coldly, as they left the table. "We'll take a drive in my car."

Sophie looked up at him mutinously. "I'd rather not, thank you."

"But you will."

"You can't make me," she breathed, so that only he could hear.

"Can't I?" His voice was just as low, and she sensed the violence behind it.

Brandt came behind them. "What's going on? What are you saying to Eve now, Edge? Can't you see how strained the girl looks? Leave her alone!"

Edge thrust his hands into the pockets of his dark trousers. "I was merely suggesting that a breath of night air might soothe her headache," he replied coolly.

"Headache?" Brandt frowned. "You've got another headache, Eve? Oh, hard luck."

Sophie folded her arms across her protectively, palms to her elbows. "I'd really rather go to bed," she declared unevenly. "Thank you all the same."

"But going to bed apparently didn't cure you last night, did it?" observed Edge.

"What do you mean?" For an agonizing moment Sophie thought he intended to expose her there and then. But obviously Edge had some other means of torment in mind.

"Well, you've got another headache," he answered mildly. "Perhaps the night air will prove a more reliable antidote."

Brandt nodded. "So long as you don't spend the time arguing with her, Edge. Take her into the mountains. The air's much cooler up there."

There was nothing for it but to agree. Sophie collected a cashmere shawl for her shoulders and then accompanied Edge down to the limousine he had driven to Port Maguerre earlier in the day.

They did as Brandt had suggested and drove into the mountains. In other circumstances Sophie would have taken a great deal of enjoyment from it. Moonlight silvered the sea glistening several hundred feet below them, and the road that wound upward was like a black snake shadowed by the tall escarpments that flanked their passage. It was much cooler up here and she shivered, but it was as much with apprehension as cold.

Edge was silent on the journey, changing gear with smooth precision, concentrating on the precipitous curves that crumbled in places beneath their wheels. He sat almost indolently behind the wheel, his long legs adjusted to the controls, the sleeves of his navy suede jacket occasionally brushing her bare arms.

At last he reached a small plateau with a narrow parking area and a handrail for tourists to stand beside to look at the view. Of course, tonight there were no tourists to occupy the spaces, nor was there a great deal to be seen in the shadowy light of the moon.

Switching off the car's engine, Edge thrust open his door and climbed out, walking lazily to the rail and resting his arms upon it. Sophie saw the flare of his lighter as he lit a cigar, but she remained where she was, stiff and nervous, unable to anticipate why he had brought her here. The silence was quite unnerving in itself, and she wished he would come back to the car and say what it was he wanted to say. It was useless to pretend that what had happened between them last night was anything more than a source of annoyance to him, and whatever happened she must not let him see how easily he could hurt her.

At last he left the rail and came back to the car, sliding into his seat beside her with negligent ease. Then he switched on the interior light and studied her pale features.

"Well?" he said. "When is she leaving?"

"Leaving?" Sophie blinked. "Leaving Trinidad?"

"That's correct. Full marks for comprehension. When does she plan to leave?"

Sophie's hands gripped tightly together in her lap. "I – I don't know. I – I can't force her to go –"

"*Like hell!*" Edge's tone erupted into violence. "Do you honestly expect me to tolerate that – that creature in my house another day longer?"

"You – you know who she is?" Sophie whispered.

"Damn you, of course I know who she is! She's James

Hollister's daughter! In every possible way!"

"Why – what do you mean?"

Edge snorted angrily. "James Hollister was an adventurer; an unprincipled rogue who married my sister to get his hands on what he imagined was a fortune! Unfortunately, he'd reckoned without my father, and when Jennifer was cut off without a penny, it must have been the heaviest blow of his career!"

Sophie gasped, "I don't believe you!"

"You don't have to. It makes no difference to me. Nevertheless, it's the truth."

Sophie was momentarily stunned. Then she began to protest: "James Hollister loved Jennifer –"

"He loved her money, or what he thought would be hers! Lord Almighty, you don't suppose I'm speaking without proof, do you? When Jennifer found out, she was sick at heart. She wrote to me, telling me what a swine Hollister was. She died when Eve was born, but I think she had no will to live!"

"Oh, no!" Sophie felt sick to her stomach. "You can't mean that!"

"Oh, but I do."

"Then – then why didn't she leave him? Come home?"

Edge stubbed his cigar out savagely in the ashtray. "Because my father wouldn't let her. What do you think this feud was all about anyway? Don't you realize that my father's guilty affection for you – for the person he imagines you to be – stems from his guilt towards Jennifer? There was blame on both sides. But Jennifer was warned. She chose to ignore that warning and look what happened! Maybe if she hadn't died in childbirth there might have been some kind of reconciliation, but it was not to be.

Whatever else my father might be, he usually was a good judge of character. He saw through James Hollister from the very beginning, but Jennifer wouldn't have it."

"Oh, God!" Sophie pressed her fingers to her lips.

"You do believe me, don't you?"

"I wish I didn't."

"Why? Because it makes your position so much less admirable?"

"No! *No!*" Sophie moved her head in a negative motion. "You won't believe this, but I didn't want to come here."

"Oh, no?"

"No." Sophie hunched her shoulders. "I wish I hadn't."

"Then why did you?"

"Would you believe me if I told you?"

"I doubt it –"

"There you are, then."

"– however, I do understand why Eve sent you here."

Sophie's eyes widened. "Why?"

Edge drummed his fingers on the steering wheel. "For obvious reasons. She guessed you were exactly the kind of girl my father would take to. Soft and feminine – not hard and brittle like she is."

Sophie bent her head. She couldn't entirely accept his judgement of Eve. She had been kind to her in the past. She had helped to get her that job at Sandchurch. Just because afterwards she had exacted some payment for that favour it did not mean she was all bad.

"So what happens now?" She looked up questioningly. "We leave, I suppose."

"*She* leaves," corrected Edge grimly.

"I can't stay here –"

"Why not?"

Sophie shook her head helplessly. "There's no point –"

"Isn't there? What about my father?"

Sophie moved restlessly. "If Eve leaves, I must leave, too."

"Why? Because she'll expect it of you? Because her little plan didn't work."

"What little plan?"

"Don't pretend you don't know. Eve only agreed to come here because the inducement was attractive enough."

Sophie tugged painfully at a strand of her hair. "Must we continue this conversation? It's obvious you know everything. Can't we leave it at that? I'll tell Eve it's no use –"

"No!" Edge was coolly authoritative. "Eve will leave; you will remain here."

Sophie gasped, "But why?"

"Because I don't want my father upset. You must have wondered why I permitted you to remain here knowing you were an impostor. There were several reasons, but only one of which need concern you. It is the most important one. For all my father's healthy, capable appearance, only two years ago he was a very sick man. He suffers from a heart disease. Two years ago he had a very severe heart attack which incapacitated him for months. Now he is recovered, but he exists on tablets, and any sudden shock – well, I'd rather avoid such a contingency."

"I didn't know." Sophie stared at him in sudden concern.

"How could you? To relieve your mind, I'll tell you

that Eve didn't know either."

Sophie breathed a sigh of relief. "And you want me to remain here until my stay is up pretending to be – Eve?"

"Yes." Edge inclined his head. "Is it so much to ask?"

It wasn't, but Sophie doubted that Eve would see it that way or that she would leave without creating a scene.

"W – wouldn't it be possible for me to pretend to be called back to London to cover an assignment?" she ventured unevenly. "Then Eve and I could leave together."

She waited for his reply with bated breath. Common sense had forced her to voice that question, common sense that told her it might be the only way to persuade Eve to leave without upsetting her grandfather; common sense that warned her that to stay on here would be madness feeling as she did about Edge . . .

She was totally unprepared for Edge's reaction to her tentative suggestion. His eyes darkened angrily, and he swung round in his seat, catching her by the shoulders, his fingers hard and biting.

"You selfish little bitch!" he muttered savagely. "You don't even have the decency to finish the job you started!"

"You don't understand –"

"Don't give me that! What's the matter? Are you afraid to stay on, is that it? Are you afraid I'll take advantage of the offer you made me?"

"Offer?" Sophie caught her breath. "What offer?"

"This one!" he snarled, dragging her towards him, putting his mouth to hers and pressing her head back against the soft leather upholstery.

"Edge!" she protested, against his lips, her palms imprisoned against his chest. "Edge, don't do this!"

"Why?" He released her mouth to bury his face in her

hair, tangling it through his fingers, kissing her nape through its silky thickness. "That's not what you said last night . . ."

Sophie tried to push him away, but it was useless. He had all the expertise of experience while she was at the mercy of her emotions. His caressing hands sent her senses spinning. She felt wholly weak and yielding. Somehow his shirt was unbuttoned and her face was crushed against his chest while his mouth probed the smooth skin of her shoulders. There was a pounding in her ears and she sensed that he was no longer in control of himself. He wanted her, and if she let this go on any longer she wouldn't care if he took her. On the contrary, there was something totally desirable in the idea of being Edge's mistress, of experiencing his lovemaking, of being possessed by the man she loved . . .

But Edge did not love her!

The words sang discordantly in her head, creating a sudden surge of self-disgust inside her. What was she doing? What was she allowing to happen? Hadn't he already made it plain that he despised her? Did she want that he should despise her even more?

With a sobbing gasp, she dug her nails into his chest and his momentary withdrawal was sufficient to enable her to press herself away from him. Staring at him with burning eyes, her mouth working miserably, she said: "Take me back to the house!" in trembling, unsteady tones.

Edge's expression was enigmatic, but she thought she glimpsed the contempt in his eyes. He moved to rest against the door at his side of the car, fastening his shirt again with lazy fingers. He didn't say anything. He just looked at her. And Sophie moved beneath his gaze like a specimen under a microscope.

When he had pushed his shirt back into his pants, he turned with slow, indolent movements to the wheel. Only then did he speak:

"You can tell Eve if she's not out of Trinidad by tomorrow evening I'll have her arrested for masquerading under an assumed identity!"

CHAPTER NINE

"HE means it, Eve, he really does!"

Sophie spoke desperately, her hands clenching and un-clenching by her sides, but Eve simply lay in bed, smoking a cigarette, apparently unperturbed by what the other girl was saying. It was the next morning, and Sophie had come to Eve's bedroom to speak to her after being turned away the night before.

"Darling, you're beginning to irritate me." Eve at last sat up and flicked ash into the tray. "What you are failing to see is that Edge is in this up to his neck. Don't you understand? He can't turn me out — expose me! Not without creating the very situation he most wants to avoid!"

"You don't mean — Eve, you wouldn't —"

"Wouldn't what? Tell my grandfather that you're not his granddaughter, after all? I would if I had to —"

"Oh, Eve!" Sophie pressed trembling hands to her mouth.

"— but I won't." Eve sighed. "Don't you see, Sophie? Edge can't allow that to happen. Not now."

Sophie turned wearily away. "So what are you going to do?"

"I shall have a few words with my respected uncle myself," replied Eve calmly, sliding a foot out of bed. "I shall explain his difficulties and mine. I'm quite sure we'll be able to come to some sort of an arrangement."

"Eve, that's blackmail!"

"Don't dramatize everything, Sophie! Edge will understand my position exactly. Leave everything to me."

"But I want no part of it."

"You've told me yourself, he expects you to stay. In two weeks it will all be over."

"Will it?" Sophie wished she could feel as confident.

The rest of the morning passed with curious normality. Piers wanted to swim, but while Sophie agreed to go down with him, she didn't go in the water. Her mind was too active to allow her to enjoy such uninhibited relaxation, and after playing about for a while, Piers joined her on the rocks.

"What's wrong?" he asked perceptively. "You look worried."

"Do I?" Sophie tried to speak lightly. "I don't know why."

"It's that friend of yours, isn't it?" persisted Piers. "She's upset you."

Sophie gasped, "Heavens, why should you think that?"

Piers shrugged. "I don't know. Just intuition, I guess. She appeared too unexpectedly, somehow. And staying here – well, I know Brandt's free with his hospitality, but really, she seemed to accept it."

Sophie bent her head. "You're imagining things."

"No, I'm not. She even has your lighter, too."

Sophie looked up. "My lighter?"

"Yes. That lighter she uses. It has your initials on it."

"Oh, I see." Sophie swallowed with difficulty. "Well – well, that's easily explained. I – er – I stopped smoking and gave it to her."

"Hmm." Piers sounded sceptical, and Sophie unwillingly recalled his preoccupation of the night before. She had wondered whether Edge had spoken to him, but it hadn't been necessary. Piers was already suspicious, if

163

for different reasons. Oh, what a tangled mess this was turning out to be!

Back at the house there was no sign of either Eve or Edge and Sophie hastily dressed for lunch, eager to find out what had happened. But when she knocked at Eve's door there was no reply and opening the door she peeped inside.

The room was deserted. There was no Eve here, and as her disbelieving eyes turned from the bed to the dressing table something momentous struck her. Where were Eve's suitcase and dressing case? Why weren't her brushes on the dressing table where they had been that morning?

Pushing the door wide she entered the room and her worst fears were confirmed. Eve's belongings had all gone. The room was no longer occupied . . .

It took her several minutes to absorb the information that Eve had departed as unexpectedly as she had appeared. But where had she gone, and why hadn't she told Sophie first?

She sank down weakly on to the bed, trying to think coherently. Eve had known how she felt about staying on here, but surely she wouldn't just leave without any warning, would she? Perhaps she had left a note, something explaining her actions, but there was nothing here.

Her own room produced no note. She had half hoped that in her haste to get along to Eve's room she had missed it, but there was nothing there and she went downstairs to lunch feeling sick and dazed. What was going on? Where had Eve gone? Only one person could provide her with an explanation, and that person was Edge . . .

But it soon became apparent that Edge was not taking lunch at home. Only Brandt, Rosa and Piers waited for her on the terrace, and she gave and apologetic ghost of a smile before sliding into her seat. On no account must Brandt suspect that anything was wrong – not now.

She was subdued during the meal and finally Brandt said: "It was a pity Miss Slater had to leave us again so suddenly, wasn't it? But never mind, I expect you enjoyed her visit in spite of its brevity."

Sophie exchanged glances with Piers, and then she said: "You know that – she's gone?"

"Of course. Edge told me before he took her to the airport. It was fortunate that she could get a flight so conveniently."

"Did – did she tell you why she had to leave so precipitately?" questioned Sophie tentatively.

"Yes. Something to do with her job, wasn't it? Still, it's good to know that you're not leaving us, Eve."

Sophie looked down at her plate. So Eve had gone as she had said she would, but had she got what she came for? Sophie shook her head almost imperceptibly. She must have done. Why else had she agreed to leave without causing any fuss? But what must Edge think of her – of them both?

During the afternoon Sophie stayed in her bedroom. Every now and then she thought she heard Edge's car cruising down the slope to the house, but when she went out on to her balcony to investigate she always found she was mistaken. Her nerves were taut and jangling, there was a dull throbbing in her temple, and her brain wouldn't allow her to think beyond the interview she intended to have with him on his return.

She lay on her bed, dry-eyed and anxious, dreading the confrontation ahead. He could hurt her so easily. She was so vulnerable where he was concerned.

She must have fallen asleep, however, for she was disturbed by someone knocking urgently at her door.

"Miss Eve! Miss Eve! Are you there?"

Blinking rapidly, Sophie scrambled off the bed and opened the door. Violet stood outside, her face working agitatedly, a pallor evident even under her darkness.

"What is it, Violet?" exclaimed Sophie in surprise. "What's the matter?"

"Can – can you come quickly, Miss Eve? It – it's Mr. Brandt. He's in his study and I don't think he's at all well."

Sophie stared at the housekeeper in horror. "What do you mean?" She ran back to the bed and slid her feet into her sandals. "What's happened to him? Where's Edge? Is he alone?"

As they hurried along the corridor and down the few steps to the main landing, Violet explained. "It was Joseph, miss, who told me. He's been to town today to get some things for me and he went in to see Mr. Brandt when he got back. He was all right then. He spoke to Joseph, asked about his trip, that sort of thing. Then about fifteen minutes afterwards when Joseph went back to ask if he would like some tea he found him slumped over his desk." Violet's eyes filled with tears. "He will be all right, won't he, Miss Eve?"

Sophie shook her head helplessly. She didn't know what to think. They hurried down the main staircase, across the hall and up the few steps that led to Brandt's study. As Violet had described, Brandt was slumped over his desk with Joseph standing rubbing his hands worriedly beside him.

Sophie hesitated only a moment and then she went to
166

the desk and put her fingers against Brandt's temple. There was a pulse, but to her terrified touch it seemed incredibly weak.

"A doctor!" she declared, trying to assume command. "Violet, can you contact a doctor?"

Violet hovered about from one foot to the other. "Yes'm. Is he going to be all right, Miss Eve?"

Sophie opened her mouth to protest – to say that she hadn't the faintest idea whether or not Brandt was going to be all right, and then closed it again. Joseph and Violet – they were like children wanting reassurance. They wanted to be told everything was going to be all right even if it wasn't.

"Of course, everything's going to be fine," Sophie stated firmly. "I think he's just fainted, that's all. Do as I say and call the doctor. Has – has Mr. Edge come back yet?"

"No, Miss Eve."

That was Joseph, and Sophie mentally chided herself for asking such a ridiculous question. If Edge had been here, he would have taken command.

Violet hurried away to call the doctor and Sophie said to Joseph: "Help me lift him on to the couch, will you?"

Joseph nodded and together they managed to get the heavy frame resting comfortably on the couch. Then Sophie sat down beside Brandt and laid her face against his chest. His heartbeat sounded a little stronger, but she couldn't be sure whether it was her imagination or not.

Joseph clasped his hands. "Is there anything I can do, Miss Eve?"

Sophie looked up. "No, I don't think so." Then she paused. "What happened? Violet said that you found him

167

perfectly normal when you came back from town."

"That's right, Miss Eve. Miss Janine was with him."

Sophie's head jerked up. "Janine Fleming?"

"Yes, miss."

"But what was she doing here?"

Joseph shook his head. "I don't know, miss."

"No, of course you wouldn't." Sophie thought hard. What could Janine have been doing at the house when Edge was not here? Although of course, she couldn't have known that he would not be here, could she? Her brain ached with the onslaught of so many chaotic thoughts. Surely Janine's visit couldn't have anything to do with Brandt's condition, could it?

The inevitable anxiety about whether Janine might have somehow learned that Sophie was not who she had said she was began to plague her. What if that was what she had come for? What if Brandt's shock at learning his granddaughter was an impostor had caused the heart attack Edge had warned her about? There were so many possibilities, and her mind couldn't begin to assimilate them all, not in this confused state.

She was still sitting beside Brandt some few minutes later when there were footsteps and Edge came into the room. His gaze skimmed over Sophie to the man on the couch, and Sophie got awkwardly to her feet when Edge came to examine his father.

To her surprise he thrust his hand into his father's breast pocket and came out with a flat box of tablets. "Get some water!" he commanded, and she ran to do his bidding, pouring some from the jug of iced water that always stood on the tray beside the other more intoxicating liquids.

168

Then he levered his father up, forcing the tablets between his lips, arousing him to consciousness long enough to swallow two. He dribbled a little water into Brandt's mouth, and to her astonishment Sophie saw his eyes flicker.

Then Edge lowered him again, and straightened, placing the glass on the tray. "What happened?" he demanded harshly. "What have you been saying to him?"

"Me?" exclaimed Sophie ungrammatically. "I – I've said nothing."

Edge considered her indignant face for a moment and then turned back to his father. "You've sent for the doctor, I hear."

"I – I thought it was best. Is – is he going to be all right?"

"I hope so. Fortunately I got here in time."

"I – I know you told me he took tablets, but I didn't know where they were – what to do!"

"Rosa would have known. Did anyone ask her?"

"I'm afraid not. Violet came straight to me."

"She would!" Edge spoke flatly.

Sophie hovered uncertainly. "I – I'd better go. Will you let me know what the doctor says –"

"I shall want to talk to you later." Edge looked remote.

"Yes. Well – well, all right. Ex – excuse me."

In the hall, Sophie was aware that her palms were wet with sweat, and the throbbing in her head had increased a hundredfold. What now?

She was still hesitating there when Violet appeared. "The doctor's on his way," she said, with obvious relief. "How is he?"

"I – Mr. Edge is with him." Sophie glanced over her

169

shoulder. "Violet, Miss Fleming was here. Joseph told me. Do you know what she wanted?"

Violet shrugged. "She didn't tell me, Miss Eve. She just said she had something to tell Mr. Brandt. I supposed it was a message from her mother, Miss Eve, about Liza."

"*Liza?*" Sophie repeated the word uncomprehendingly. "You mean – you mean the girl who – who –?"

All of a sudden she couldn't go on. She was remembering last night, the argument she and Eve had been having in her bedroom, and a certain serving girl standing outside her door, listening, overhearing . . .

"That's right, Miss Eve." Violet didn't seem to notice her hesitation. "That girl who's been such a nuisance here. Seems like she's offered her services to Mrs. Fleming, and they've taken her on."

"Have they?" Sophie felt weak. All of a sudden the pieces were falling into place and she didn't like the pattern they were making. What would Edge think when he learned this? Would he believe that she had said nothing? That if his father knew the truth Janine was responsible?

Violet was looking at her a little strangely now, her head tipped on one side. "You feeling all right, Miss Eve?" she asked, with concern. "You're not letting this trouble with Mr. Brandt upset you too much, are you? Mr. Edge said not to worry. Mr. Brandt will be fine."

But Edge would say that just as she had said it earlier. He couldn't know for certain. Shaking her head, she managed to placate Violet and after the African woman had left her she went slowly into the lounge. What was she going to do? If Brandt really had had a heart attack, if he died . . .

But no, that couldn't happen, she told herself desperately. She couldn't have been a party to such a thing. He *had* to get better, whatever he had been told.

A speck of something wet fell on to her hand and she realized with a sense of dismay that she was crying. The tears were streaming down her cheeks, and the aching emptiness inside her seemed more than she could bear. What was she going to do? How could she stay here now if Brandt knew the truth? He might never want to see her again. And as for Edge . . .

She shook her head, rubbing fiercely at her face to dry it, stopping the flow of tears. Crying was weak and cowardly. She had come here of her own accord, no one had actually forced her to do so, and it was up to her to face the consequences. But right now . . .

On impulse, she went out into the hall and finding the blue file beside the telephone which held the personal numbers known to the family she pressed the letter F and came up with the Flemings' telephone number. She dialled the figures carefully, refusing to think about what she was doing in case second thoughts prevented her from going ahead, and when a maid answered she asked to speak to Miss Janine Fleming.

"Miss Fleming's not at home, miss," replied the maid, politely. "Shall I bring Mrs. Fleming to the phone?"

"Oh, no – no, that's all right," Sophie was beginning half relieved at the reprieve, when she heard voices at the other end of the line and presently Howard's deeper tones came to her ears.

"Eve? Eve, is that you?"

Obviously Howard hadn't yet learned of her true identity, thought Sophie, relaxing a little. "Yes," she replied. "I – er – I wanted to speak to Janine, but it wasn't important."

"Won't I do?" Howard joked. Then he sobered. "You sound upset. Is anything wrong?"

"Well, yes. Brandt had a bad turn a short while ago. We're waiting for the doctor to come now."

"My God!" Howard sounded really concerned. "Is there anything I can do?"

"No, thank you, I don't think so. I – I must go. I think that's the doctor arriving now."

It was. Violet appeared and hustled him up the stairs to Brandt's study and Sophie wandered aimlessly through the morning room and on to the terrace. She wondered where Piers was. He'd probably gone out in the dinghy. He had asked her earlier on, in the morning, but she had refused. She wished he was here now. His uncomplicated presence was exactly what she needed.

Presently she heard voices in the hall and going to the door of the morning room she saw that the doctor was leaving again. The briefness of his visit seemed to point to nothing too serious, but she daren't speculate until she knew for certain.

Edge accompanied the doctor down to his car, and Sophie crept up the stairs to the open door of the study. Brandt still lay where she and Joseph had put him, his eyes were still closed, but he seemed to be breathing quite normally.

She was descending the stairs again when she encountered Edge.

"He's sleeping now," he advised her uncompromisingly. "He'll probably sleep for several hours. But there's nothing to worry about."

"Oh, thank God!" Sophie clasped her hands together with relief.

Edge's expression was enigmatic. "I suggest you go and have some tea. You look as though you could use some. I'll speak to you later."

Sophie nodded and turned away. At least Brandt was not going to die, she thought, drawing deep trembling breaths. And after all, that was the most important thing.

She was dressing for dinner, her thoughts still as chaotic as ever, when one of the maids came to tell her that there was a telephone call for her.

"For me?" Sophie was surprised. Who could be calling her?

She took the call in the hall, lifting the receiver carefully, putting it to her ear reluctantly. "Er – Eve Hollister here. Who's that?"

"Someone who knows you're not Eve Hollister," remarked a female voice that she recognized at once as belonging to Janine. "I understand you were calling me earlier this afternoon."

Sophie sank down weakly on to the bottom stair. Janine's words had stunned her and for a moment she could think of nothing to say.

"Well?" Janine spoke again. "You must have known that sooner or later you'd be found out."

"You – told – Brandt?" Sophie could hardly formulate the words.

"Not yet. But I shall unless you make arrangements to leave immediately."

Sophie felt drained of energy. "You want me to leave?" she breathed incredulously.

"That's right. Tomorrow if possible." Janine sounded impatient. "I should have guessed sooner that the way you looked at Edge –" She broke off abruptly. "Anyway, I know now, and I'll not hesitate to expose you for the impostor you are! I don't know why you came to Trinidad, I don't know how you got Brandt's address, unless Jennifer's real daughter is behind this. But you'd better start packing or the St. Vincentes will have something else to get steamed up about."

The phone went dead and Sophie realized the other girl had hung up on her. She had made her threat and Sophie had no doubt in her mind that she meant what she said. She would tell Brandt. She, unlike the rest of them, had nothing to lose.

There was another telephone call during dinner and Sophie's nerves tensed as Edge went to answer it. But when he came back his face was merely thoughtful and he bent to swallow the remainder of his wine, but did not sit down again.

"I've got to go out, Rosa." He addressed himself to his aunt. "There's been some trouble in town with some of our men. I'll have to go and sort it out. I'll see you later." His eyes flickered over Sophie as he said these words and she realized he was warning her that she would not escape their interview.

But what was the point? she asked herself after he had gone. Whether or not he demanded that she should stay and finish her time here didn't matter now. Janine meant what she said. She would tell Brandt, and Sophie had to decide whether the hurt of her staying or going would be the greater.

When the meal was over Piers disappeared about his own business and on impulse Sophie left the house and went down the steps to the stone jetty below. There was quite a breeze this evening, and it blew her hair about her face and caused bumps of gooseflesh to appear on her skin. But at least the air was fresh and clean and blew away the cobwebs of intrigue and anxiety.

The unusual swell was causing the dinghy and the motor launch to bump more heavily against their moorings, and Sophie walked towards them slowly, watching their movements absentmindedly. But then she saw that the ropes mooring the dinghy were loose. Either Piers hadn't secured them fast earlier or the wind had had a hand in their loosening, but definitely the dinghy was on the verge of being swept away from the jetty.

Sophie forgot her own troubles for a moment and bent to catch the rope. The wind and a sudden rush of swell almost swept off her feet, but she managed to regain her balance and bent to tie it up again. However, it was then that she discovered that the mooring ring had rusted through and that was how the dinghy had got loose in the first place.

She looked round helplessly, holding on to the rope, trying to see some other fastening suitable to moor the boat, but there was nothing. Her only hope was to fasten it to the launch's mooring and hope that it would hold them both.

Her hands had become cold, however, and the rope was suddenly jerked from her fingers by the impatient wind. The dinghy bobbed about like a cork and the rope disappeared into the water a few inches out from the jetty.

"Oh, damn!" Sophie stared at the small vessel frustratedly. If she had never come down here she wouldn't have known that the dinghy was loose, but she had, and now she didn't quite know how to leave it. She could hardly start yelling up to the house for assistance with Brandt lying asleep in his study, so what could she do? Leave it and hope it wasn't carried away by the tide? Or try to rescue it?

She looked down at her pleated skirt and long-sleeved blouse. If she started messing about in the water they would be ruined. On the other hand, the bra and pants she had on underneath were no less daring than her bikini and far more serviceable.

On impulse, she stripped off her skirt and blouse and jumped into the water. It struck her as chill, but the sensation soon passed. It was still much warmer than the sea back home.

She managed to reach the dinghy in a couple of strokes and grasped the line. Then she turned and tried to pull it back towards shore. But unfortunately it was a land wind and it drove against the dinghy, gathering strength in its ruffled sails and causing Sophie's arms to ache. It was terribly frustrating, particularly as she was beginning to feel really cold and knew that sooner or later she might have to give up the attempt.

And then cramp struck her, an agonizing pain in her left leg which made her gasp and let go of the rope and momentarily submerge. She came up frightened and fighting for breath, unable to envisage any way of making it back to shore. Instead, she grasped the side of the dinghy and hauled herself over, straining her aching back to collapse in a heap in the bottom of the boat.

It was wonderful to be out of the water, to feel the cramp begin to release her muscle, but the momentary respite was subdued by other sensations. She was very cold, her teeth were chattering, and the shore was slowly but definitely receding.

She knelt up in alarm. Whatever was she going to do?

Even if she knew how, she doubted whether she would dare to raise a sail in this wind, and the dinghy might quite easily be carried out to sea.

She realized her only chance lay in diving over the side and making a desperate effort for the shore. If she remained where she was, anything might happen. The dinghy might capsize and then . . .

Giving her leg a final brisk massage, she stood up and again, without giving herself time to change her mind, dived over the side and swam towards the rocks. The sea washed over her head several times and she had to spit out mouthfuls of water, but she kept on going, ignoring the tentative twinges that came to trouble her. The rocks had never seemed so far, and eventually she acknowledged she was not going to make it. Her only chance was to reach the Point, jutting out of the water a few yards to her right. It looked stark and uninviting with little about it on which to cling, but she had no choice.

At last she reached it, dragging herself up out of the water as her strength gave out on her. The rough surface of the rock tore at her fingers, but somehow she levered herself upward, first with handholds and then by her feet as they sought and found crevices worn away by the constant movement of the salt water.

Near the top there was a narrow ledge, wide enough for her to wedge herself on to, and she rested her head wearily back against the rough edge of the rock. At least she was safe for the moment. This part of the Point was never completely submerged and as soon as she felt stronger she would try for the shore. She was cold and tired and not a little nervous, but for the moment her other troubles were forgotten.

CHAPTER TEN

SOPHIE awoke to the sound of voices, urgent angry voices that drifted across the water to her in waves, like the rise and fall of the swell. The swell. . .

She blinked rapidly and tried to move. Every bone in her body ached with weariness, for although she had been dozing, there had been no sense of relaxation. On the contrary, she had tried to stay awake, but the coldness made her want to close her eyes. She had known she should have been trying to swim the distance between the Point and the shore, but the water looked so churned up and uninviting and she had told herself she would wait just a little longer.

But now – now there were voices, which meant people. Surely someone would see her out here.

And yet how could they? It was dark, there was no moon tonight and what little light there was would not illuminate a still form resting against the rock face, not unless she could attract their attention by some other means.

Wincing as her body protested at being subjected to such exhaustion, she managed to move away from the rock face and look desperately towards the shore. She could still hear the voices, but they seemed to be moving away, and if she didn't act quickly they would be gone.

"H – help!" she called faintly. Then more strongly: "Oh, please – help me!"

The wind seemed to carry her voice away, disguising her weakness within its strength. The voices receded further and panic added a touch of hysteria to her frenzied calling: "Help! Oh, God, I'm here! *Help me!*"

There was silence for a moment and her worst fears seemed realized, but then the talking broke out again and she realized whoever it was was coming back.

"Help!" she called again, her voice hoarse and cracking. "I'm on the Point!"

"*Sophie!*" It was Edge's voice. "Sophie, can you hear me?"

"Yes," she called back, her voice weakening. "Thank goodness you've heard me!" And then her voice broke altogether and she began to sob, harsh, choking sobs that racked her whole aching, freezing body.

"Keep calm! I'm coming out for you!" Edge shouted, and she heard him shouting commands to whoever it was that was with him. She heard the engine of the motor launch being started and presently its steady rhythm as it began to cross the water between herself and the shore. All the while Edge kept shouting to her, encouraging her, but she was scarcely conscious of his approach. Shock and fear and exposure had all played their part and she was no longer in control of herself.

As the launch neared the rocky promontory Edge shouted again: "If I throw a rope, can you catch it?"

Sophie tried to pull herself together. "I – I'll try."

Edge tossed the coil towards her. It snaked down beside her and it was quite a simple matter for her to pick it up. But her fingers were too numb to hold it and it slithered helplessly away.

Edge didn't ask her a second time. Instead he brought the launch in close and crouching low, sprang across the two feet of water to land on the ledge beside her.

"Oh, Sophie!" he muttered, and now there was a break in his voice. "I thought you'd killed yourself!"

Sophie looked up at him tremulously, struggling to get to her feet, and uncaring of her wetness he gathered her closely against him, burying his face in her neck.

"Dear God," he groaned, "you're chilled to the bone! Come on! It won't be much longer now. I've got to get you back."

Sophie would have been quite willing to remain where she was in Edge's arms. It was where she belonged, and who knew whether his reactions were motivated purely by guilt or by some deeper emotion.

She didn't remember much about the journey back to the house. Edge had Joseph with him and he wrapped Sophie in blankets while Edge steered the craft. Then, once they were on the jetty, Edge swung Sophie up into his arms and strode towards the steps with her.

"I – I'm much too heavy," Sophie breathed against his neck. "Edge, I can walk."

"I doubt it," muttered Edge in reply, and then proceeded to ignore any further protest she might make.

Violet met them at the door of the house, her black face mirroring her concern. "Oh, Mr. Edge, you've got her! Is she all right?"

"She will be," remarked Edge flatly. "Go ahead and get some hot water into the bath."

"Yes, sir, Mr. Brandt."

Violet scurried ahead up the stairs, Edge following her, seemingly unperturbed that he was still carrying the burden of Sophie's weight. In her room he allowed her to stand on her own two feet and she immediately realized that she was wearing only bra and pants.

180

Her arms crossed themselves across her body, but Edge merely looked impatient. "Get your bath!" he advised briefly. "Soak as long as you like. There's no hurry."

As Sophie stepped into the perfumed water that Violet had run for her she asked the time.

"The time, miss?" exclaimed Violet, in surprise. "Don't you know it's nearly two o'clock!"

"Two o'clock in the morning?" Sophie couldn't believe it. "But – but why isn't everyone in bed?"

Violet gave her an old-fashioned look. "Now, miss, that's rather a leading question, isn't it? What with Mr. Edge half out of his mind looking for you, sending Mr. Piers over to the Fleming house to see whether by any chance you were there."

"I – I was missed?" Sophie slid down into the heated water. She was just beginning to feel warm again. "But – when?"

"About eleven o'clock, I guess. When Mr. Edge got back from town. He wanted to see you and when you couldn't be found he seemed convinced you'd run away."

"Run away?" echoed Sophie.

"Yes, Miss – er – Sophie, isn't it?"

Sophie shot upright in the water. "How do you know that?"

"Why, everyone knows, miss."

"Everyone?" Sophie's cheeks paled. "Brandt – that is – Mr. Brandt, too?"

"Everyone," came a voice from the doorway, and turning Sophie saw Edge draped lazily against the jamb. Immediately she slid down under the soapsuds again, her cheeks colouring scarlet.

"Now, Mr. Edge, you didn't ought to be in here," re-

181

proved Violet, picking up Sophie's discarded garments and putting them into the dirty linen basket. "You'll be able to talk to her time enough."

"That I will, Violet." Edge sounded very certain of that. "But hurry up, will you? I'm impatient."

He turned and left them and Sophie hastily began to soap her arms. Her head was spinning with what she had heard, and she didn't dare to speculate why such news had not made Edge angry instead of so – so – She shrugged helplessly. She didn't quite know how to describe him, but right now anger was not part of his make-up.

After Violet had towelled her dry with one of the huge apricot towels, she slipped on a chiffon nightdress and wrapped a towelling bathrobe over it. Violet smiled a little mischievously at this obvious effort to conceal herself, but she went away quite happily once she was sure that Sophie had everything she needed.

Sophie was seated at her dressing table combing her hair when the door opened again and Edge appeared. He came into the room familiarly, closing the door behind him, and immediately her heart began to pound. She put down the brush and watched him approach her through the mirror, and presently his hands descended on her slim shoulders and he bent his head to put his mouth against her neck.

Sophie raised her shoulder to his touch, and then he straightened again and put a little distance between them, drawing out some cigars and lighting one. She noticed that his hands were not quite steady as he raised the flame of his lighter to the tip of the cigar and then he turned away, walking slowly across to her balcony.

Her heart skipped a beat. What now? Was he about to

revert back to his sardonic self?

But when he turned there was no mockery in his face. On the contrary, it was wearing a curiously strained expression. "You feel – all right?" he enquired quietly.

"I–I'm fine." Sophie rose from the stool and stood looking at him across the width of pale carpet. "I'm sorry if I was a nuisance."

"A nuisance?" He raised his eyes heavenward. "Oh, God, if only you knew what an understatement that was!"

"I'm sorry."

"Why be sorry? I deserved more. God, when I found you were missing, I – I –" He shook his head. "Well, never mind that now. How the devil did you get out there?"

"I was trying to bring the dinghy back."

"The dinghy?" He looked blank. "You took the dinghy out?"

"No I didn't take it out exactly. The mooring is rusted through. The dinghy was loose. I tried to bring it back."

"I see." He raked a hand through his hair, his eyes glittering strangely. "So that was why you took off your clothes. Hell, when I found them, I really thought – I really thought – " He turned away abruptly, as though unable to continue, and Sophie felt a surge of compassion run through her.

But before she could say anything, he went on: "You see, I discovered this evening when my father awoke that he had learned that you were not Eve, after all."

Sophie stiffened. "And – was that why – why –"

"Why he passed out, you mean? No. He'd just forgotten to take his tablets, that's all," he replied, turning back to her.

Sophie felt a wave of relief sweep over her. "But – but who told him? Janine said –"

Then she broke off as Edge's eyes narrowed, but he would not let her get away with it. "Yes?" he prompted. "Janine said what?"

"Oh – oh, nothing." Sophie bit her lip.

"You think Janine told him, is that it? Did she threaten she would?"

"She may have done. I don't remember." Sophie moved uncomfortably.

"Well, for her sins, it wasn't Janine."

"Then – then how?" Sophie was unable to understand.

Edge assumed a wry expression. "He opened a cable that was addressed to you. He thought it might have been something urgent. Joseph brought it when he came back from town, and you weren't around, so . . ." He shrugged. "I believe *you* sent that cable!"

The cable!

Until that moment Sophie had forgotten its existence. The day she had sent it Eve had arrived and consequently all thoughts of the communication she had sent to her in London went out of her mind.

She stared helplessly at Edge and he went on: "You did send it, didn't you? I can see it in your face. Thank heavens you did!"

Sophie was confused. "But why?" she whispered.

"Don't you realize that cable exonerates you? It was obvious from its wording that you had only agreed to come here because you thought Brandt was practically a dying man. That you had no part in the attempted extortion!"

Sophie spread her hands. "But how did it get here?"

"By the usual processes. Eve wasn't to be located in

184

London. Obviously she must have told her neighbours she was going away. The cable, being an urgent kind of communication, was sent on here."

"I see." Sophie nodded. Then she had a thought. "But how do you know I didn't send it for just those reasons?" she persisted.

Edge gave her an impatient look. "Did you?"

"No."

"I believe you. I believe my instincts. You're simply not that kind of a person. I guess I knew that all along, but I needed to have it forced on to me before I would actually accept it. I'm sorry."

Sophie shrugged awkwardly. "That's all right."

She didn't quite know how to take what he was saying. Earlier he had been distraught and she had imagined probably a lot more into his behaviour that had actually been expected. Perhaps it was only guilt he felt, guilt at having baited her for so long, at having treated her with such contempt. Whatever physical attraction he had felt for her he had despised himself for it every inch of the way.

Now Edge was speaking again: "You may be surprised to learn that Brandt was beginning to have suspicions that you were not Jennifer's daughter."

Sophie listened intently. "Yes?"

"Yes. You know how it is – one forms a picture of someone from their letters. It's possible to read a person's character from the letters they write, and my father has had a good deal of experience in dealing with people. He was beginning to realize that you were avoiding the discussion which he had expected you to demand. The motives behind Eve's acceptance of his invitation. But you see ..." Edge took a step towards her, "... my father had begun to be fond of you, of the person *you* were, and he was dreading having to seek answers which might destroy the relationship between you."

Sophie's heart beat fast. "If only I'd known . . ."

"If only we'd all known," commented Edge dryly. "Things would have been so much simpler. But there, if Eve hadn't devised this ingenious charade none of us would ever have met, would we?"

"I suppose not." Sophie looked down at her hands. "But I must tell you that there was another reason why I was persuaded to come here."

"Another reason?" Edges brows drew together ominously.

"Yes." Sophie moved uncomfortably. "You see, there's to be an actors' summer school in Rome later this year, and Eve knew that I'd never be able to afford such a thing on my own, so she offered to help me . . ." Her voice trailed away miserably. "I suppose that makes me almost as bad as she is, doesn't it?"

Edge said nothing for a moment and she hurried on: "Your – your father told me you took Eve to the airport this morning – I mean, yesterday morning."

"I did." Edge's expression softened slightly. "I should think right now she's back in London."

"But how did you – I mean, was she willing to leave?"

"She was – eventually."

"You mean – you mean you gave her what she wanted?"

"Of course not." There was a trace of his old arrogance back in his voice again. "I give money to nobody without wishing to do so."

"But she said –"

"She said a lot of things," Edge interrupted her. "Including regaling me with that story about you agreeing to come here so that you could go to Rome. She omitted the part about the actors' summer school. She gave me some garbled story about some man you were interested in who was working there –"

"Oh, no!" Sophie stared at him in silence.

"Oh, yes."

"But she was my friend –"

"With friends like her you don't need enemies," remarked Edge dryly.

"No." Sophie digested this. "Oh, well, I suppose that's everything, isn't it? I mean – well, Brandt knows the truth and he'll get over his disappointment in time. Eve – well, Eve will manage, she always does. And me, I'll go back to the playhouse in Sandchurch. If you're ever in England, you must look me up –"

Her voice almost broke then and she had to turn away, taking deep breaths, trying to calm herself. Time enough to cry when he had gone. All the time in the world, in fact.

She heard him move and presently his breath fanned the back of her neck. "This summer school," he said quietly. "Does it mean a lot to you?"

Sophie cleared her throat. "It was an idea, that was all," she replied.

"If you want to go, I'll finance you." Edge's voice was low but distinct.

Sophie caught her breath, swinging round to look at him in amazement. "Why – why should you do that?"

Edge's eyes were narrowed. "I feel you've had a raw deal. I'm doing what I can to put it right."

Sophie bent her head, shaking it determinedly. "No,

thank you all the same. I don't think that would be a good idea."

"Why not? There'd be no strings attached."

"I'm sure there wouldn't, but I'd rather – I'd rather not take anything from – from you –"

"Why? Why not?" Edge caught her by the shoulders, shaking her a little. "God, I know I've been a pig in the past, I know I've hurt you, but I thought you were scheming little minx and every time I got near you I despised the feelings you aroused in me –"

Sophie stared at him. "Don't you mean lust?" she asked tremulously.

Edge gritted his teeth. "All right. You have a right to say that. You have a right to hate me. But can't you see, I'm trying to make amends?"

Sophie bent her head. "Brandt won't expect me to stay the rest of the month now, will he?" she murmured. "I'd think it would be best for both of us if I left tomorrow – I mean, today, don't you?"

"No! Damn you, I don't think it would be best at all."

A muscle was jerking beside Edge's mouth and his hands gripping her shoulders were beginning to hurt her. Sophie turned her head.

"I'm tired now. I'd like to rest. Will you please go?"

"Oh, Sophie – Sophie," his groan was muffled against her neck. "Don't go cold on me. I don't want to leave you. I love you!"

Sophie's hands pressed against his chest trembled. "Edge –?" she began unsteadily, and then his mouth was on hers, and for several minutes there was silence in the warm, lamplit room.

Sophie finally drew back a little to look at him, her fin-

188

gers caressing his temple. "Edge?" she whispered again, "what did you say?"

Edge's mouth caressed her cheek. "You heard me," he murmured, holding her a little more tightly against him so that her body was moulded to his. "And I think you know I mean it."

Sophie blinked. "Then why do you want to send me away?"

Edge sighed. "I don't *want* to send you away. I just feel I should."

"But – but you must know that – that I –"

"That you imagine yourself in love with me?" queried Edge gently. "Yes, I had a good idea you did. But you're so young, so inexperienced, while I – well –" He shrugged. "You know the kind of life I've led, and I've been married into the bargain."

"Yes. Piers told me about that."

"Did he?" Edge's expression was wry. "Oh, well, so you know about me. But you – you have all your life ahead of you. If you went to this summer school you might do very well – you might even become famous. Who knows? Surely that's what I ought to do for you – not this." And he bent to kiss her again.

Sophie's arms curved round his neck. "Oh, Edge, Edge, you don't know how happy you've made me! And as for acting – well, that's strictly for unmarried women."

"You are assuming I want to marry you, then," remarked Edge, rather dryly, and she flushed. But he shook his head with self-derision, and added: "As if I'd settle for anything else! You've got under my skin, my darling, and when there's no cure, one has to keep on taking the medicine!"

Sophie's eyes twinkled. "Such medicine! Will you mind?"

Edge slid the bathrobe off one shoulder. "I'll try not to," he promised. "Hell, why did you bother putting this thing on?"

Sophie responded rapturously to his touch and then she remembered his son. "There's still Piers," she whispered against his neck. "Do you think he'll mind?"

Edge buried his face in her hair. "I shouldn't think so. He's fond of you himself. And naturally my father will be delighted."

"Will he?" Sophie was doubtful. "He didn't expect you to marry again."

"Until this evening," commented Edge, with a smile. "I think he had a pretty good idea that you meant more to me than he'd imagined when I stormed through this place looking for you." He shook his head. "God, when I think of you out on that rock, at the mercy of the elements –"

"Don't think about it," urged Sophie softly, and Edge seemed to take her advice . . .

MILLS & BOON FIESTA!

25 Favourite titles now available once again

MILLS & BOON are bringing 25 of their favourite titles back into print. If you would like to obtain any of these titles please contact your local stockist or in case of difficulty please use the order form overleaf for your requirements, enclosing your remittance.

FREE! YOUR COPY OF OUR MAGAZINE OF MILLS & BOON ROMANCES

Complete the coupon below and send it to MILLS & BOON READER SERVICE, P.O. Box 236, 14 Sanderstead Road, S. Croydon, Surrey CR2 0YG we will gladly send you, post free, your own copy of our magazine – "Happy Reading" together with our complete stock list of over 400 Mills & Boon romances.

☐ Please send me the free Mills & Boon romance magazine.

☐ Please send me the titles ticked (Please include 2p per book p & p, 10p outside U.K.)

I enclose £...(No C.O.D.)

Name.. Miss/Mrs

Address ....

City/Town ....

County/Country.................................. Postal/Zip Code...............

LOOK OUT FOR THESE TITLES

All priced at 20p. See over for handy order form. Please tick titles required.